Counting Down to Christmas!

R. A. Hutchins

Warmest Wishes

[signature]

ISBN: 979-8-6995-4228-4.

For Michael,
Thank you for always encouraging me to follow my dreams.
I love you.

CONTENTS

'Blessed is the season which engages the whole world in a conspiracy of love.'

Hamilton Wright Mabie

1. A Talented Performance

'Goodnight, Ella,' Doctor Jeffries shouted back as he headed out the door, into the snowy evening.

'Goodnight,' Ella replied, absent-mindedly, desperately trying to type the last of the audio notes before turning her computer off for the night. There was only one patient left, old Mrs Emery, who was in with Dr Marsden now. Her nephew, the local vet, sat patiently in the waiting room, as he always did when he brought her for her ever-more-frequent visits.

Ella looked at him surreptitiously from under her glasses. He was certainly a fine figure of a man, tall and broad, with laughter lines around his eyes and a smile that always held a hint of fun. Ella looked forward to seeing him, though she had barely spoken more than two words to him in months. Especially now that the new computer sign-in system had been installed.

Impatiently, Ella typed the last sentence, sent the patient's notes to the printer, and began her nightly routine, shutting down her files methodically, and finally turning off her PC. Strictly speaking, she should wait until the last consultation of the day was finished, and all patients had left the building, but tonight was December 22nd, and Ella had a whole list of jobs to complete.

Not present buying or baking, no, living alone meant that Ella had finished wrapping and posting her family gifts earlier in the month, and all should (fingers crossed) have arrived at their destinations by now.

No, Ella had something far more stressful to attend to.

A month ago, the deputy chairperson of the local parish council had been in for her monthly appointment. Mrs Juniper was a thick-set woman, with a terrifying air of confidence, who simply never took no for an answer. She was always the first port of call when the parish council wanted to enlist someone to volunteer for a village activity. So, on that fated night in November, Ella had been enjoying a rare moment of quiet in the surgery when Mrs Juniper had bustled in, ten minutes early for her appointment. She was always punctual, but never early, as Mrs Juniper hated to be kept waiting. This change in routine made Ella look up from her typing.

'Ah, Miss Tait, I hoped to see you here!' gushed Mrs Juniper, in her most obsequious tone.

Where else would I be on a Tuesday afternoon? thought Ella to herself.

'The parish council and I wanted to offer you a very special position!'

Ella's heart sank. She had never learnt how to say no to people, let alone people like Mrs Juniper, who was far too reminiscent of Ella's own mother for her liking.

'Um, special position?' Ella inquired hesitantly.

'Yes, dear,' Mrs Juniper continued, more slowly now, as if talking to a child, 'the role of village talent show organiser has unexpectedly become available and we couldn't think of anyone better for the job!'

Ella had heard that Mr Potts, who normally organised the annual Christmas event, had decided to retire from volunteering this year, following a particularly loud argument with Mr Hobbs, leader of the parish council for the past eighteen years.

Ella lost track of Mrs Juniper's endless prattle, only tuning back in when she heard, 'so we'll see you tomorrow evening, at half past seven at the village hall, for the first meeting,' as Mrs Juniper strode off into the doctor's room.

Oh no, Ella thought to herself. At the ripe old age of thirty-six, and with no husband or boyfriend, Ella tried to keep herself to herself. She was a classic introvert, and didn't socialise in village life unless it was something that she had a particular interest in. Village talent shows were not on that, admittedly limited, list. But now she had no choice.

Things had gone downhill from there, with the majority of the organising falling on Ella's shoulders. Apparently, the rest of the parish council were more 'front stage than back stage,' and refused to lift a hand to help, as they needed to be 'perfecting their acts.'

And so here she was, on December 22nd, wondering why on earth anyone would think December 23rd was an acceptable date for a whole-village activity. *Surely people had their own festive chores to attend to?* Ella wrapped her scarf tightly around her neck to ward off the chill, said goodbye to Neil Emery (who warmed her up right there and then with one of his gorgeous smiles) and headed out in the direction of the village hall.

Expecting to find the decorating already started in the hall, Ella was shocked to find only the caretaker, ancient Mr Wilden, who was struggling to carry a small step ladder. Rushing forward, Ella caught the step ladder in one hand, and Mr Wilden in the other, as he lurched forward unsteadily.

'Are you ok? Where is everyone?' Ella asked, in one breath.

'Who?' Mr Wilden retorted.

Smiling her thanks, Ella propped the old man against the wall and went into the big, empty hall. Six large boxes lay deserted in the middle of the room, beside a huge, fake spruce, its bare, gnarly limbs pointing off in a multitude of directions. Ella dropped her bags, and sat down beside the pile, which had clearly been unceremoniously dumped there for her attention. There was a strong smell of musky damp, from wherever this lot had been stored.

Two of the younger – and by that, they were perhaps in their late fifties – *parish council members should have been here this afternoon,* thought Ella, and those high school girls I promised the Starbuck's vouchers to.

Ella put her head in her hands. Her shiny brown hair (a blessing from her mother's Italian heritage) fell over her face, and her large, chestnut eyes brimmed with unshed tears. Ella wasn't one to give in to fits of emotion. Not since her breakup with Cheating Simon four years ago, had she even contemplated sitting sobbing. No, her default setting was to be practical, to search for a solution. Now, though, with a whole hall to decorate, and no help, Ella couldn't see a light at the end of the tunnel. Certainly not one that was adorned with baubles and twinkling fairy lights, with a big Ho Ho Ho thrown in for good measure.

Just as the tears began to fall, Ella's phone buzzed. Scrabbling around in her handbag, she eventually found the offending item. It was a text message from Mrs Juniper:

Ella, dear, Mr Potts has just announced that he won't be dressing up as Santa either this year. That man!

Having no children of her own, Ella had to admit that Santa Claus had not even featured on her list of preparations for the event. She vaguely remembered that, as a child, she had walked up onto the stage at the end of the show to receive a gift and a hearty laugh from Father Christmas, but it hadn't occurred to her that she needed to organise one for this year.

The tears fell more swiftly now, until Ella was hiccupping out huge, messy sobs. The release felt good, and Mr Wilden was partially deaf, so Ella continued unabashed.

Until, that is, the sound of someone pointedly clearing their throat caught her attention.

Pushing her bob back out of her eyes, and taking off her steamed-up glasses, Ella was horrified to see Neil Emery in the doorway. What on earth was he doing here?

'Um, hi,' Neil said, shifting from one foot to the other uncomfortably, 'My Aunt said you might need some help?' *Ah yes, Mrs Emery was on the parish council, of course she was, she went every week religiously for the free tea and scones.*

'Help, yes well, we have the hall, it needs... a lot of work. Then there's the programme to be printed, the props checked for every act, the music to be given to Miss Prest, the church organ mistress, the lighting....' it was like verbal diarrhoea and Ella couldn't stop herself. She heard the words coming out of her mouth, but felt powerless to rein them in. Embarrassed, she looked down at the floor, still sniffing from her earlier breakdown.

'Here,' Neil walked over, offering her his arm which Ella hesitantly accepted, letting him help her up off the floor. His shirt sleeves were rolled up and he seemed to be without either jumper or coat. The butterflies that Ella felt on touching his bare skin were quite off-putting, though thankfully he seemed to attribute her lack of balance to her having got up too quickly.

'Thank you,' Ella said, more than a little flustered, realising that she had held on to him for considerably longer than was polite. She reached down to her Waitrose bag-for-life and brought out a large clipboard, on which was attached a very long, typed 'To Do' list.

'I'd be very grateful for any help,' she continued, allowing herself for the first time to look into his deep, brown eyes.

Careful, Ella, you could lose yourself in those, Ella silently cautioned herself. Neil's unwavering smile put Ella at ease, though the little laughter lines around his eyes did nothing to calm her butterflies.

At that moment, a large scuffle in the hallway caught their attention, quickly followed by five larger-than-life teenage girls bursting through the doorway.

'Sorry, Miss,' one announced loudly, chewing gum while she spoke, 'We went home first to get changed then to the shop for sweets, then Sam saw the boy she's gotta crush on so we…'

'Well, at least you're here now!' Ella interjected. She looked through her list, assigning jobs to the girls, and only then realised that Neil was gone.

Oh well, Ella thought, *having his help was too good to be true anyway*. Resigning herself to disappointment felt like Ella's natural state of being, she was so used to it.

She needn't have doubted his commitment, however, as Neil soon reappeared from the large, outdated kitchen with two cups of coffee, a jug of juice, a plate of biscuits and some glasses on a tray.

'We can't have the workers going hungry!' he said jovially, as he placed the tray down on the nearest trestle table and ate two Rich Teas, in two huge gulps.

Those had been Ella's dad's favourite biscuits too, she recalled, and the unexpected memory brought a happy feeling. Usually, Ella tried to shove down any thoughts of her father. His passing had been the single hardest event of her life, and she still succumbed to grief whenever she allowed herself to think of the friendship they had shared when she was a girl. Normally fleeting, this time the happiness remained as Ella began setting up and decorating the tree, with Neil sticking closely to her instructions.

'I'm not very good at this kind of thing,' he admitted sheepishly, 'I don't normally decorate my cottage because I spend Christmas at my Mum and Dad's – for my sins!'

Ella smiled, a real and genuine smile, that was uncommon for her as she rarely let her guard down enough to relax in company.

'I think you're doing great,' she gushed, 'Just maybe turn that Santa the right way up!'

The sudden thought of Santa brought Mrs Juniper's text flooding back in all its import. 'Oh no,' Ella muttered.

Sensing the change in her mood, Neil suggested they take a break. The schoolgirls were hanging bunting and fairy lights around the room, apparently engrossed in a hilarious story about a boy, a maths book and a broken chair. Mr Wilden had announced that he was off for the night and would come back tomorrow with his grandson to lay out the chairs for the audience and the tables for the refreshments.

'It's all in hand,' Neil reassured her, seeing Ella's expression of doubt, 'Come on!'

Thinking they were just going into the kitchen, Ella let Neil lead her out of the hall. She was surprised, though, when he grabbed both of their coats off the pegs in the hallway and held the front door open for her.

Shrugging into her coat, Ella was hit by a draught of icy cold air. It had started snowing heavily, and the ground was covered in a beautiful layer of soft white, reflecting in the glow of the old-fashioned streetlamps on Front Street. They turned the corner, with the village green laid out before them, a perfect square of white like the icing on a Christmas cake, when a blast of icy wind knocked Ella backwards slightly. Without a word, Neil took her hand and placed it in the crook of his arm. It nestled cosily, and Ella felt a warmth that spread from that limb throughout her entire body.

'Nearly there!' he shouted above the roar of the weather.

To be honest, at this point, Ella would have followed Neil anywhere, Hugging close to his side, the village idyllic in its wintery attire, she was the happiest she had been in a long time.

They reached the vet surgery, and Neil produced a fat, overladen keyring from his coat pocket. They walked down the side of the old building, and in through the back door.

The warmth hit them, as if they were stepping out of the airport on a summer holiday.

'We need to keep the temperature up for our patients!' Nick laughed, as Ella quickly removed her coat before she began to melt. 'I needed to check on Buster here, and I thought you might like to meet him.'

Neil bent down to one of the cages and brought out the cutest black Labrador puppy that Ella had ever seen. One of his legs was in a blue cast.

'Buster here thought he'd try going for a walk by himself, in the traffic,' Neil explained, shaking his head. He's lucky it was just Doc Jeffries on his pedal bike and not the farmer's tractor!'

He handed the eager puppy to Ella. His injury didn't seem to have dimmed his enthusiasm, and he began covering her in excited kisses. Ella laughed, caught up in the moment. She looked up at Neil, and the look in his eyes was unmistakeable. Gently lifting the puppy back into his cage, Nick was equally cautious as he stroked Ella's cheek with his fingers. Ella dipped her head into his palm, and they stood there looking at each other, as time stood still.

Slowly, very slowly, Neil lowered his mouth against hers, and Ella met him with an eagerness she had thought she no longer possessed. Their kiss was slow and sweet and impossibly long. Pulling away, Neil looked at her deeply, as if questioning her total acquiescence.

As if he could have a doubt after what just happened, Ella thought to herself. Nevertheless, by way of reassurance, she reached her mouth back up to his again. This time, their connection was not as slow and shy. The heat between them grew, until they were kissing passionately, his hands running up and down her arms in slow seduction, her hands stroking through his hair. Ella felt her heart soaring as her hope was reborn.

'I've waited a long time to do that!' Neil admitted, coming up for air, but still holding her close.

Ella blushed, 'Really?' she asked, 'I didn't know!'

'Not even when I brought my aged aunt to the doctor's surgery for every slight ailment?' Neil laughed.

Ella's blush deepened, as he leaned down to find her willing lips again.

It was at least half an hour later when the couple, now holding hands, returned to the church hall. Ella was struck by how festive and welcoming it now was and thanked the girls for their effort as the five left, still chattering incessantly. They seemed very happy with the promise of a Starbuck's voucher each, and Ella considered it money well spent.

Ella and Neil sat on the edge of the little stage, the Christmas tree standing proudly behind them, and kissed again.

'Now I've started, I can't seem to stop!' Neil said sheepishly. Ella really didn't mind and showed him so.

'I guess Santa came early for us this year!' Neil joked.

SANTA!

'Oh my goodness,' Ella whispered, 'I totally forgot, I still need a Santa Claus for tomorrow night.'

She looked at Neil, as realisation dawned on her that he'd make the perfect, jolly gift-giver.

Neil agreed, in return for her promise that she'd have dinner with him after the event.

'How could I refuse?' Neil asked, taking hold of both of Ella's hands and kissing them each in turn, 'The show must go on!'

2. CARIBBEAN CHRISTMAS

The sun was beating down, the waves were lapping up, and Mark felt great. Beyond great, he felt fabulous. Wasn't that was Dr Heinrich had said? *Speak it into realisation*, or some other such crap.

The main thing was that here, on Paynes Bay Beach, there was no hint of Christmas. Not the smallest bit of tinsel or stray bauble. No expectations, no incessant calls from his mother, no pitying glances and no insincere well-wishes.

Just beautiful sand, great beer, and miles of peace and quiet.

Just what the doctor ordered, Mark thought sardonically.

To be fair, it was great to be outside again, he'd spent too long cooped up in a stuffy room at the military hospital. Marc adjusted his position in the deckchair slightly. Sitting too long in one spot made his remaining leg go numb. Oh the irony – one leg that was half missing but wouldn't stop itching, and one that was real but kept losing feeling. *Happy Days!*

Three weeks, and four days back at home with his parents, while he was 'convalescing', after spending seven months already in hospital (you gotta love sepsis), was three weeks and three days too long with his parents. Mark had felt slightly admonished, when his father had taken him aside on his final evening with them and told him he was, 'selfish to leave your mother worrying,' but this was not enough to change his mind and at eight hundred hours the next morning he had boarded a plane to Barbados.

He'd been here just under a week and Mark was confident he'd made the right choice. He may not be travelling the world in the military any more, but there was no reason why he shouldn't enjoy a bit of R&R in a beautiful location. Right?

The remaining part of Mark's leg (he refused to refer to it as a 'stump') began to throb and he had to concede defeat. He'd deliberately left his prosthetic at the hotel. That thing was heavy as hell, and just as hot. Nope, he didn't want to sit here letting that piece of metal heat up like a frying pan. So, he'd ditched it earlier and hopped to his favourite spot. Pushing himself up with his well-toned arms, Mark reached under the chair for his crutches.

He had only taken a few moves towards the hotel, a mere two hundred metres away, when his crutch caught on a hidden stone under the sand and Mark fell forward. Completely flat on his face, getting a mouthful of sand for his troubles.

Dignity in shreds, Mark struggled to sit up. The sun shone down from directly above him, so even when seated on the sand, his chest heaving, Mark had to shield his eyes, his sunglasses having flown off in the fall. He struggled to contain the anger which, since the incident, was always bubbling just under the surface. The inclination to hurl his crutches across the sand was so strong that he had to count to ten, peppering it with a different swear word between each number. Thankfully, his time in the army had served him with a ready supply of those!

'Are you looking for these?' a voice asked smoothly. Mark's heart sank. *Why did someone have to come along, at the exact moment of his embarrassment? And of all people, why did it have to be a hot girl in a yellow bikini?*

'Thanks,' Marc said gruffly, taking the glasses from her and giving out, he hoped, clear signals that he wished to be alone.

'Can I help you up?' the girl asked in a perfect English accent.

'No. Thank you!' Mark responded, his voice sounding harsh even to his own ears, 'I'll manage.'

'Really?'

Why won't she take the hint? Mark asked himself, as he tried, unsuccessfully, to haul himself up again. He swore repeatedly under his breath.

She waited, patiently, until finally he had to concede defeat. Refusing to say anything, simply lifting his hand in her direction, Mark allowed the stranger to get him on his feet (well, foot) again.

Balanced once more upon his crutches, Mark shrugged off her hand. Looking closely, he saw that she really wasn't a 'girl', rather a woman in her twenties.

'Caitlin,' she said, holding out her hand in greeting. Mark gave her hand a cursory shake, mumbled, 'Mark,' and began his slow trek back to the hotel again. The woman, however, must either have skin as thick as a rhinoceros, or just simply be ignorant, Mark decided, as she insisted on walking alongside him, at his slow, loping pace, all the way to the foyer.

'I guess you're not much of a conversationalist!' Caitlin said, clearly trying to lighten the tone and relieve some of the tension. It fell on deaf ears, and Mark shouted, 'Thanks,' as he made his way to the lift.

Later that day, after a much-needed nap (he had now finally accepted that it was better to give in to his body's need for rest, rather than continue fighting it), Mark made his way downstairs to find some food. Thankfully, the hotel provided all-inclusive stays – Mark's medications meant that his appetite was often non-existent. He simply ate when he felt hungry, so the lunchtime buffet was by now long-gone. *Never mind,* Mark thought to himself, *I'll order a burger to eat on the balcony.*

Going to the reception desk to arrange his meal, Mark was surprised when Alesha the Service Manager on duty (and his personal favourite) handed him a short, handwritten note. It read:

Great to meet you, Grumpy! Fancy a drink on the terrace this evening? C

Mark was in no doubt that the note had been left by Caitlin. That woman was infuriating. And gorgeous. Infuriatingly gorgeous. Yes, that summed her up perfectly.

The note hadn't stated a time, so Mark left his room at seven hundred hours exactly and took the lift down to the foyer. I'm only going because I have no other plans, he reassured himself. He'd taken another shower because he needed one and put on fresh clothes and aftershave for his own pleasure, of course. It had nothing to do with his drinking partner.

Stepping out onto the large hotel terrace from the air-conditioned interior of The Sugar Cane Club Hotel, Mark was hit by a wall of heat. His hands quickly became damp and slippery on his crutches. Looking around for Caitlin, Mark couldn't spot anyone vaguely matching the picture of her in his memory – beautiful face, long, curly brown hair, toned legs… 'Hi Mark!' A tap on his shoulder brought Mark back from his hot musings.

Caitlin came around to face him. She was even more stunning than he remembered, all curls and tan. She was no longer wearing the bikini, sadly (*had he really expected her to be?*). Instead, she had on a pair of very skimpy, white denim shorts and a black halter-neck top, which was cropped to display her bare, toned midriff.

What am I even doing here? Mark thought to himself, suddenly hit by a crisis of confidence. *This is the type of girl I used to chase. What would she see in me now? A cripple.*

Caitlin stood patiently, watching him thoughtfully.

'Hi,' Mark's voice came out as a croak, 'Um, thanks for the message. I'm sorry about earlier today. I was a jerk.'

'No worries,' Caitlin reassured him, 'I think your manly pride had taken a battering,' she added in a teasing tone.

'Well, that's one way of putting it!' Mark agreed. His arms and legs were aching and he desperately needed to sit down, but he certainly wasn't going to announce that fact.

Caitlin was still studying him closely and seemed to sense his growing discomfort. 'It's so hot,' she said, 'let's find a table in the shade.'

And with that she walked off towards a far corner of the terrace, with Mark following behind.

Armed with a beer and some sugar cakes, sheltered under a large parasol and sitting on a padded chair, Mark finally began to relax and enjoy Caitlin's company. He learned that she and her family holidayed in a villa here every Christmas, coming across from their home in Kent. She had graduated a couple of years before from the University of Aberdeen in Scotland and was working in London as a Beauty Technician on the Bobbi Brown counter in Harrods.

Mark could definitely see why she'd be a perfect fit for that role!

Pausing in her chat, Caitlin looked to Mark and asked, 'What about you?'

Mark froze, his beer halfway to his mouth. He dreaded this question. His trauma was still too raw to speak freely about. Not just the IED explosion in Southern Afghanistan that had shattered his foot and shin, but also having to leave the army. The only job he'd ever wanted. Now, at twenty-nine, he was just a small fish, floundering against the tide, missing a fin.

Of course, he couldn't say any of this to a stranger he barely knew, he hadn't even been able to share it with his best mate back home, who he'd known since primary school. Mark had studiously avoided James' calls and texts in the few weeks he was back home. He knew he was being a dick about it, but he figured he was allowed some slack.

Mark lowered his beer back to the table and let out a long sigh.

Caitlin said nothing, but reached over from her seat next to him and put her hand over his. This small gesture was anything but small to Mark. He felt a lump form in the back of his throat. *What the hell?* He thought to himself, *I can't cry right here, and especially not because a girl touched me.*

Caitlin started to rub her thumb in small circles around the back of Mark's hand. Daring to lift his eyes to meet hers, and the pitying look he knew he'd find there, Mark was surprised to see no such expression. Instead, Caitlin's eyes brimmed with understanding, and a special twinkle. What was that? Laughter? No, perhaps a zest for life.

She began talking again, but didn't remove her hand from Mark's, still tracing its gentle path over his skin.

'When I was a girl,' Caitlin said, 'Maybe six or seven, my best friend fell from a tree we were both climbing and was badly hurt,' she paused, taking a sip of her cocktail. 'He ended up in a wheelchair, he couldn't ever walk again. His back was broken, you see.'

Mark could think of nothing useful to say, so simply nodded. The effect of Caitlin's touch, and the beer mixed with his meds, was wreaking havoc on his crotch, and it was slightly disconcerting. That part of him had been dormant for a long time. So long, in fact, that Mark had assumed it was another bit of him broken forever. *Come on, man!* he checked himself, *she's talking about an accident, you knob!*

Mark refocused on Caitlin's story.

'He was fine,' she continued, 'until we were teenagers, and his disability became too much for him to bear. He tried to kill himself,' she whispered the last sentence.

Now it was Mark's turn to show understanding. He turned his hand palm upwards, to take her hand fully into his. Then he began massaging Caitlin's palm the way she had been doing for him.

'Don't worry,' she whispered, 'I found him, we got him help, he's doing great now, married and everything,' she rushed the last part of her story as if keen to get the explanation finished.

They sat in comfortable silence and looked at each other for a long while. Neither wanted to break the moment.

Eventually, the waiter came over to offer them more drinks. The sun was a beautiful setting orb on the horizon, and the lowered temperature was a perfect balmy blanket over them.

'Yes, please,' Mark answered for them both, 'and perhaps some food.'

'Certainly, Sir, I will bring a selection of Chef's finest dishes for you and your beautiful lady!'

Caitlin laughed politely, modestly. Whether from being called beautiful, or his lady, Mark wasn't sure.

The evening progressed in easy conversation, until it was completely dark and they moved into the hotel's main lounge. A piano player was tinkling classics in the background, and the huge Christmas tree and twinkling festive lights gave the room a magical quality.

When Caitlin excused herself to go to the bathroom, Mark gave himself a silent talking-to. *What are you doing here, mate? It's not like this can lead to anything. She's...*

Caitlin's return halted his inner monologue. He watched as every man in the room turned to look at her as she walked past. A vision of loveliness, and yet Mark had the impression that Caitlin had little idea how lovely she really was.

As she sat back down and flashed him a gorgeous view of her legs, and her smile, Mark was stunned again by the twinkle in Caitlin's eyes. He'd seen it before in other girls, though to be fair it was normally when they'd had too much to drink, and it was certainly back when he was still whole. Caitlin, however, had only had two cocktails and a handful of mocktails all night, so she probably wasn't even tipsy. Mark, on the other hand, was starting to regret his three pints of beer. The crutches were hard enough to navigate in a busy room, let alone when the world was spinning.

'Let me help you back to your room,' Caitlin offered, as if reading his mind. Mark couldn't tell if it was a sympathy offer given his current state, or a genuinely flirty gesture. Either way, he said 'yes' immediately.

They held hands walking to the lift, with Mark using his crutches under his other arm. When the lift dinged on his floor, and they reached his room, Mark paused, unsure where to go from here.

Caitlin, however, had no such debate in her mind. She effectively pinned Mark against the closed door, leaned forward and touched her lips to his. No demanding, no reading between the lines, just a simple kiss was offered, and Mark eagerly accepted.

It was like fresh water after a drought, and Mark couldn't get enough. Their kiss lasted much longer than was probably appropriate in a public place, so Mark quickly unlocked the door with his key card and they went into his room.

They both sat down next to each other on the small velvet sofa in the bay window. The atmosphere had changed, and Caitlin seemed to have lost her confidence.

'It was a lovely evening,' Mark said, happy to give her a get-out clause. Heck, he probably needed that just as much himself! This was unchartered ground since his accident, and he had no map.

'I'm not normally like this,' Caitlin blurted out, 'I don't want you to think that I do this kind of thing regularly, because I certainly don't. I had the same boyfriend for three years at university, and not even kissed anyone since. But when I saw you on the beach earlier...'

'Please don't mention that,' Mark interrupted defensively.

'No,' Caitlin explained, 'not when you tumbled. Earlier, when you arrived, and were sitting on your deckchair, and when you rested by the water and...' she began to blush a deep shade of pink. Even the tip of her nose had the rosy hue, and Mark found it extremely sexy.

'You mean you were watching me all morning?' Mark asked, in a cheeky tone, grinning.

'Yes, well, you were a very... um... pleasant sight!' Caitlin stopped talking, aware that she was probably sounding like a teenager with a crush.

Mark leaned in to kiss her, just to put her out of her discomfort, he told himself. They kissed with a passion that blew Mark away. He ran his fingers through her shiny, long curls and felt her running her hands up and down his chest.

Caitlin pulled away and dotted small, sweet kisses around his jawline, reaching his ear. She whispered, 'This is... well amazing... but I don't want to lead you on. I don't do one-night stands. Or first date sex.'

Mark couldn't have been more relieved. He realised he should probably sound at least a bit disappointed, but his wide smile said it all.

'Caitlin, that's fine. Perfect even.'

'But,' Caitlin continued, hesitantly, running her fingers through his nervously, 'I definitely don't want the night to end now. We could have a sleepover? If you like? I love cheesy Christmas movies!'

'I'm actually not a great fan of Christmas at the moment,' Mark admitted, before realising that he was totally missing the point. 'But, to be fair, my festive season has certainly become a lot more cheery in the past few hours!' He gave Caitlin a cheeky wink. 'Your choice first, but nothing with elves, they creep me out!'

An hour later, they were both snuggled under the blanket, with popcorn and cookies and hot chocolate. 'It's not Christmas chocolate if it doesn't have cream and marshmallows!' Caitlin had told the room service attendant.

Mark's sudden panic that no-one had seen his wound was short-lived, as Caitlin was unbelievably sweet about it. Not that he'd thought for a minute she wouldn't be, but nobody needed to see him changing the dressing on that thing.

'Don't worry,' she said, 'I'll go into the bathroom and slip into this t-shirt of yours while you get yourself sorted.'

Job done, thought Mark contentedly, as they curled up to watch the first movie, 'Love Actually'.

With Caitlin's head resting on his chest, her breathing matching his, Mark decided that maybe the holidays weren't so bad after all.

3. COMING HOME

Shona tapped her fingers on her knee impatiently. The taxi was stuck in Bristol's rush hour traffic and, as per usual, she'd left it to the last minute to get to the airport. It was raining heavily, that kind of winter rain that is icy cold and more like sleet. It slanted sideways and hammered off the window next to her, blurring Shona's view of the world outside.

Pulling up outside the airport, Shona paid the driver and wrestled her case, laptop bag and handbag into the terminal. There seemed to be handles and straps everywhere, and she was bending down as she ran, trying to sort them.

Thump. Shona bumped into something large and stationary. Surprisingly soft though. Looking up, she couldn't keep the shock from her eyes.

'David!'

'Shona!'

They stared at each other incredulously. Any intention to apologise died on Shona's lips when she saw the unimpressed look on his face.

Extending her gaze, Shona saw that she had in fact landed at the queue for the Newcastle flight, where there were six people ahead of them.

'What are you doing here?' David asked.

What a stupid question! Shona thought to herself. She bit her tongue. Now was neither the place nor time for an argument, and she'd had a long day at school so her patience was wearing thin.

'I'm flying up to see my parents before Christmas,' was her tempered choice of retort.

'Hmm, me too,' David replied.

It shouldn't have come as a surprise to either of them, since home was where they had met some thirty-odd years ago. To be travelling on the same day, on the same flight a week before Christmas – well, that was just pure bad luck.

'How's Katie?' David asked, bringing Shona back to the present.

'Oh, she's fine. Back from Manchester, but she has exams straight after Christmas so she didn't want to make the trip. She has her boyfriend staying, you know the one, Rick, he's a medic too, though I doubt any anatomy studied while I'm away will be helpful in their exam!' Shona raised her eyebrow suggestively, in an expression which David knew well.

'Ah yes, Rick,' he said, a tone of displeasure evident.

'Is she still coming to you on Boxing Day?' Shona asked. Their daughter, although now twenty, still split her time between both her parents. They had only been separated for fifteen months, since she started university in fact, so to her not much had changed, except that David now lived in Devon.

Their necessary pleasantries dealt with, the two stood in silence, until the awkwardness became too uncomfortable. *How can two people married for so long become strangers?* Shona asked herself. The answer, she knew, was a painful truth to bear. She had not spent much time pondering it over the past couple of years, preferring to revert to her typical method of self-distraction – work. Shona was proud to be the Principal of an academy of schools in Bristol, all with Ofsted Outstanding reports and long waiting lists. The truth of their break-up, Shona knew, lay more with her than with David's breakdown, but she had decided there was no point in dwelling after the fact.

Clearing his throat awkwardly, David asked, 'Are your parents well?'

'Yes, thank you, I think so. I talk to them regularly, but I haven't actually seen them since Easter. Dad says Mum is getting a bit forgetful, probably just her age. Yours?'

'Yes, dad's ok. Still missing mum, still struggling with loneliness. He's sharp as a knife still, so he misses human contact. I set up Meals on Wheels to be delivered, so at least I know he's eating properly now.'

'Ah, yes, good idea.' Shona replied, watching the queue creep forwards at a snail's pace.

David let her check-in first, ever the gentleman. She wasn't sure whether to wait for him or not, but decided to head straight to security. *Given the time, and in case there's a queue,* she justified to herself.

A quick stop in Duty Free to buy some Talisker for her dad and chocolates for her mum, and Shona was at the gate just in time for the plane to be called. She deliberately kept her eyes down, not wanting to spy David and have to subject either of them to further awkward conversation. Luck was not on her side, however, when finding their seats led the pair straight back to each other.

'Second row from the front,' they both said in tandem, by way of explanation, as they realised with a sinking feeling that they were in fact sitting next to each other for the whole flight. When they were first married, they had decided this was the spot on the plane they preferred. Every holiday as a couple, and then as a family of three, they had tried to book this row. It probably shouldn't have been a surprise that they would both continue the habit now.

'At least it's a short flight,' David mumbled, though not quietly enough to not be heard.

Hand luggage stored, they settled down in their seats. It was only a small plane and was crammed full. Shona was secretly relieved to not have to squash in beside a total stranger. She hated flying. It was a necessary evil which she endured, but her preference would always be to drive if possible. There simply hadn't been the time to do that now. She was only having a flying visit up North, two nights, back on Sunday to prepare for Monday's work. Shona planned on working right up till Christmas day, though her schools had already closed for the holidays.

The take-off could at best be described as 'bumpy'. Shona gripped the armrests until her knuckles turned white. Once airborne, the turbulence continued, causing her to shake with fright. She wasn't aware of the tears streaming down her cheeks, so focused was she on the breathing techniques she had been taught.

David was very used to Shona's phobia of flying and looked across to see the beautiful woman, who he still loved, breaking down trying to cope alone. Instinctively, he reached out and rubbed her knee. Shona didn't acknowledge his touch, but neither did she push him away, so David took this as a small win. They had never got around to getting divorced. Of course, solicitors had been consulted in the early days of their separation, but since everything had been amicable, no blazing rows or hurtful actions, divorce wasn't high on their list of priorities. David was glad.

The plane levelled and the shaking in the cabin petered out. Shona's attention came back to the present, and she looked down at the hand gently rubbing her knee. She didn't have the heart to ask David to stop. She wasn't even sure if she wanted him to. The familiar touch was comforting and stirred up feelings she had tried to bury under a mountain of work. When the air hostess came along with the trolley, and David took his hand away, Shona felt strangely bereft.

Seeing no point in being silly about it, they agreed to share a cab. Their parents only lived half a mile apart at the coast – Shona's parents in Tynemouth and David's dad in Cullercoats – so it made sense to travel together.

Arriving at her destination first, Shona said goodbye to David, reaching across to peck him on the cheek. She had no idea why she'd done that and put it down to tiredness and relief at being off the plane. *We were married for twenty-three years,* she told herself, *of course it's natural to kiss him on the cheek.*

But was it natural to miss him this much?

Shona's arrival was greeted by the usual excitement from her mum and dad, who were always eager to see her and normally fussed over her for the whole of her stay.

'So, where's my gorgeous granddaughter? Mum asked, when they were all ensconced in the sitting room with a cup of tea and some Battenburg cake.

'Home from university, but spending a few days with her boyfriend before he goes home to Cornwall for Christmas,' Shona said.

'Ah, a boyfriend!' Dad winked and gave a knowing nod, 'Was that David I saw in the back of the cab?'

'Yes, we happened to be on the same plane, that's all,' Shona answered defensively.

'David!' Mum shouted, as if she had only just remembered his existence, 'Where is he? Is he parking the car?'

Shona shot her dad a worried glance.

'No, dear,' dad said patiently,' remember Shona and David don't live together anymore.'

'Since when?' Mum asked crossly, clearly resenting the insinuation that she was mistaken.

Dad looked over at Shona for help, shrugging his shoulders, and whispering, 'Mum struggles with her memory sometimes.'

Shona was shocked. Her dad had mentioned on the phone that mum was getting forgetful, but she had imagined forgetting bread on the weekly shop, not that her only daughter was no longer married.

'Is there anything else happening?' Shona asked, pointedly looking at her dad, but keeping her tone light and airy.

'No, no,' said dad quickly. Too quickly, thought Shona.

'It was funny when I put my glasses in the oven to warm them up though, wasn't it dear!' Mum chuckled to herself, 'they were so cold on my face, you see!'

'She didn't actually turn it on,' Dad added quickly.

Shona felt sick. Her parents were in their seventies, so she knew they were aging and physically couldn't do as much as they used to, but she had not thought her mum's mental health had deteriorated so badly in such a short space of time.

'We've left the tree for you to decorate,' Mum carried on unawares, 'You always like that, don't you!'

Shona hadn't helped them decorate a tree since she married David when she was almost twenty-five. However, she didn't see any point in mentioning that now.

Half an hour later the small carriage clock on the mantle chimed ten, and her parents began to yawn. Shona was glad of the excuse to head upstairs and said a quick goodnight to them both.

She trudged upstairs to the guest bedroom, thankful that it had an en-suite bathroom, so she could shut herself away and not need to come out again till morning. It was all too much to process. Her head throbbed, her limbs ached, and all she wanted to do was stand under a hot shower and block out the world for ten minutes.

Coming out of the shower, winding her towel around her wet hair like a turban, Shona saw a message had popped up on her mobile phone.

It was from David:

Laptop left in taxi. Have it here. Will drop round tomorrow. D x

The thought of seeing David tomorrow – calm, practical David – was, to Shona's surprise, a big comfort. Particularly after the revelations of her conversation with her parents.

Shona went straight to bed yet, despite her exhaustion, she tossed and turned most of the night. Memories of her mum over the years came to her from nowhere, from being a small girl running out of school into her mother's waiting arms, to seeing her in the auditorium at her university graduation and in the church at Katie's christening. It all seemed a bit too painful right now. Then there were the other memories. Of her and David. In sixth form together at the Valentine's ball. At their wedding reception in the Grand Hotel on the sea front. On their honeymoon in Salzburg. The list went on. She had not had such a disturbing night in a long time.

The next morning, Shona was woken with a cup of tea from her mum.

'Thank you,' she said, 'you shouldn't have.'

'I always wake you up!' her mum said happily.

Shona sat up and looked at her phone. Eight o'clock. Wow! She never normally slept past six. Picking up her cup, Shona took a gulp, and almost spat it back out again. Looking into the mug, she saw it was full of tepid water with a single teabag floating in the middle. 'Oh God,' Shona said, perhaps to the Man Himself.

She hurried to get dressed and rushed downstairs. David had texted to say that he and his dad would be round at eleven, and perhaps they could all have a walk on the beach together?

A walk along Longsands had always been one of the highlights of their visits, so Shona understood why David would want to recreate it. At eleven on the dot they arrived just as Shona had finished decorating the small, imitation tree.

'David!' her mum squealed, rushing to give him a hug, 'Let me look at you!'

David gave Shona a querying look, but smiled down at mum with affection and accepted her warm welcome graciously, 'Hello, Mavis!'

He had brought his dad, Donald, who shook hands with Shona's dad. They had known each other for a very long time – since before Shona and David became an item – and were firm friends.

'I was wondering if I could have your help with my suitcase?' Shona asked David pointedly, 'the lock seems to be stuck!' She motioned in the direction of the stairs.

'Yes, you young people catch up, and we'll have a cuppa!' her mum said, disappearing into the kitchen, with dad hot on her heels.

David seemed understandably startled at the request, but followed up the stairs without comment.

Closing the bedroom door behind them, Shona burst into tears. This was completely out of character for her, and she surprised herself as much as her husband.

David said nothing. He reached out and pulled her into his arms, rubbing her back and letting her sob into his chest. Shona reached her arms around him and nestled her head into the crook of his neck, where it had always belonged. They stood like that until she had cried herself out, and then moved to sit on the bed next to each other. David took hold of Shona's hand and waited patiently for her to get whatever it was off her chest.

'My mum,' Shona began haltingly. She told him everything that had happened from the moment she arrived. David listened, nodding in understanding and asking occasional questions.

He had always been such a great listener, Shona wished she had returned the favour and listened to him more in the months after he had been made redundant and sunk into depression. She had organised GP appointments for him, found him a Cognitive Behavioural Therapy course, and a counsellor, but had she actually taken the time to just listen and hear him, the way he was doing with her now?

Sadly not, she thought. She wasn't proud of the fact that his being at home had made her stay out longer at work. The day she had come home to the note, saying he was moving to Devon to turn his art hobby into something more professional, she had simply felt numb. There had been no big scene, no grand admonishments. Just silence from them both in the end. They were communicative and cordial where Katie's visits were concerned, and that had been it. Over twenty years of a happy marriage, and Shona hadn't even fought for it. She was honest with herself for the first time since the break-up – it was her biggest regret and failure in life.

Realising she had drifted off into her own head, Shona looked at David, really looked at him, into the gentle, grey eyes that were so familiar and so unknown at the same time. Without letting herself debate the wisdom of her action, Shona leaned forward and kissed him. He kissed her back without hesitation, eagerly and tenderly and now they were both crying. It felt like coming home.

Not in a rush to join their parents downstairs, the pair let their reignited passion guide them and reconnected again on every level. Shona felt two years of pent-up tension and sadness leave her body, and the release was immense.

As they returned a while later to the sitting room, Shona and David were surprised to find their parents all grinning like Cheshire cats. 'Did we miss something?' Shona asked, hoping they hadn't been too loud, and didn't look too dishevelled.

'We've been talking,' her dad said, 'with Donald, and we've hatched a fantastic plan!'

Shona and David were shocked to learn that this idea involved David's dad moving in with Shona's parents and selling his small flat. This would certainly help with Donald's loneliness, and also give Shona's dad some help with looking after her mum.

'We have even had time to write a list!' dad said eagerly, clearly relieved. At the top of the list, Shona saw the line,

Get a doctor's appointment for Mavis!

'As wacky as it sounds, it may just be an excellent idea!' David said, rubbing his hand up and down Shona's back protectively. 'Then we won't have two separate sets of parents to see when we next visit!'

With that he kissed Shona's cheek, to a round of applause from their family.

4. MESSAGE FROM AN ANGEL

Maisie stood proudly at the front of the stage, her blonde curls bobbing up and down as she swayed from foot to foot. Every ten seconds or so, she reached up and adjusted her shiny, golden halo nervously. The mummies and daddies were all sitting in the big hall, looking at them. She had already spotted her Daddy sitting near the front, and had shouted, 'Hello! I'm here!' to make sure that he had found her. Everyone had laughed a bit at that and Maisie felt unsure why. Anyway, it was fine now, she just had to wait for Joseph to say, 'It's a baby boy!' to Mary and then it was her turn to speak. Why on earth Miss Bhatti had chosen Felix to be Joseph, when he kept picking his nose, was a mystery to Maisie. She had asked Miss Bhatti and she had replied simply, 'Everyone has their perfect part, Maisie.'

Maisie had agreed. Miss Bhatti was so clever. Like how she had given Maisie this special part, and now she was an angel just like Mummy! Daddy had cried a bit when she told him that she would be an angel in the Reception nativity. She had thought she'd done something wrong, but he said he was just so happy to have his Maisie-Moo, and he'd given her a big, squishy hug that made her giggle! Yes, Miss Bhatti was very clever, Maisie thought she was the best teacher in the world.

Then her big moment came. Daddy had told Maisie that Mummy would be watching from above her. She squinted her eyes really tightly and looked up at the ceiling, but couldn't see the lady from the photos. Everyone was looking at her. Maisie began, 'I bring you…' and stopped, unsure of the next words. She began to panic, her bottom lip trembling. Miss Bhatti, from her position kneeling in front of the stage, whispered, 'big news of great joy,' and Maisie relaxed, shouting out the familiar line so that everyone could hear.

She was sure that Mummy would have heard, too. Daddy said that Mummy would be very proud of Maisie. Maisie knew what 'proud' meant. She was very proud of Daddy. He was a doctor and he made people better every day. She didn't understand why he hadn't made Mummy better, but she didn't want to ask him yet.

So happy with herself, Maisie gave a little curtsy and danced off the stage with a flourish.

Seeing his little girl standing there, her chubby legs encased in white sparkly tights, and her home-made dress adorned with silver tinsel and white feathers thanks to his mum, Craig felt a huge swell of love, that started in his heart, and ended in a lump in his throat. He coughed to hide the emotion and waved at Maisie, who was now sitting on a bench to the side of the stage. She waved back and blew him a kiss.

Craig knew that he was going to be late for his first clinic, as he hadn't anticipated how long it would take to get thirty excited four-year-olds onto a stage, in the right places, and remembering their lines. He didn't care, Cathy, his nurse specialist, would handle things till he arrived, as she always did. Nothing was more important to him than Maisie. She was his precious guardian angel.

Clara, Felix's mum, turned from her seat in front of him, and mouthed, 'She's so sweet!'

Craig nodded and smiled his thanks. He liked Clara – a single parent like himself, they often gravitated towards each other at events like this, where normally both parents would be in attendance. Felix and Maisie had attended the same pre-school, so they had known each other for a few years now.

After the show, the parents were asked to leave through the back door of the hall, while the children stayed in their final places on the stage, singing another encore of 'Away in a Manger.' *This is a good idea, to try to avoid any separation upset,* Craig thought, but he knew how it would pan out with Maisie. He had tried to explain to Maisie the previous evening, that she had to stay at school after her performance, as she had her Christmas party there that afternoon, but Maisie was having none of it.

'But, you will need a kiss goodbye, Daddy,' she had said, her big blue eyes round and intense, 'to set you off for work like we always do.'

So, here he was, trying to disappear out of the back door without a scene. He had waved at Maisie, blown her a quick kiss, and turned his back, even though his heart was aching.

About five seconds later, Craig heard the wail. He recognised it instantly, and his paternal instincts had him running back, pushing through the crowd of other parents, onto the stage, where he scooped Maisie out of Miss Bhatti's arms and sat down on the low, wooden bench with her on his knee, kissing her squashy, wet cheeks.

'You'll be fine, my Maisie-Moo,' he reassured her, 'You'll have your special party, with your new dress that's in your backpack, and Granny will collect you at home time. When Daddy picks you up from Granny's we'll go for ice cream to celebrate your amazing nativity performance!'

Maisie started to look placated. Her sobbing turned to the occasional sniffle.

'With snowflake sprinkles?' she asked, referring to the white chocolate, snowflake shapes that had become her new festive favourite topping.

'Of course, Honey.'

Standing her back on her feet, Craig walked Maisie to the back of the line of children quietly filing out of the hall. Giving her a final kiss on her forehead, he hurried out the other way, smiling to the teaching assistant who was about to shut the back door.

Craig was surprised, but not at all disappointed, to see Clara waiting for him at the school gate. They often walked back to their cars together, chatting about their children and the juggle of working full time and parenting solo. He appreciated Clara's straightforward, no-nonsense approach, and her advice was always exactly what he needed to hear.

Today, however, Clara seemed a bit out of sorts. Nervous, even.

'I was wondering,' she began, without any preliminary conversation, 'if you and Maisie would like to come to Alnwick Gardens with us this Saturday? They have a festive maze, a Santa's grotto, and a Snowman parade. Felix is desperate to go, he has a thing about snowmen at the moment. I thought we could wrap up warm and take a flask of hot chocolate?'

Craig was surprised, as they had never met up socially, but didn't let it show on his face.

'That's a lovely idea,' he said, 'I struggle sometimes when it's just me and Maisie, to drum up the level of excitement she expects for events like those! I'm sure Felix will help with that!'

'He certainly will!' Clara replied, looking her normal, happy and relaxed self again. 'See you then! I'll text you about the arrangements!' And with that she was gone, getting into her Mini Cooper.

Craig hurried to his own car, a new spring in his step. Wherever could that have come from?

The rest of the week dragged slowly, until Saturday finally arrived. Maisie was beyond herself with excitement, jumping up and down at the car door,

'Hurry, Daddy! Hurry, they'll be waiting!'

They drove the five minutes to Clara and Felix's house, where an equally excited Felix was already waiting outside, complete with matching snowman bobble hat and scarf.

The journey to the gardens took less than half an hour. The two adults sat in the front chatting, while the little ones pointed out of the window and had their own conversations.

'Did you know that my Mummy's a real angel?' Maisie asked Felix, with an air of authority.

'Wow! A real one?' Felix replied enthusiastically.

'Yes! A real one!'

'When can I meet her?'

The adult conversation had ceased as soon as Craig heard Maisie mention Marta. His wife had been diagnosed with terminal, aggressive cancer at four months pregnant. She had stoically refused any chemotherapy or surgery until after Maisie was born at thirty-six weeks into the pregnancy. His beautiful, brave Marta. She had only survived to see Maisie turn one month old.

He was about to intervene and answer Felix's understandable, but awkward question, when Clara interjected, 'Maisie's mummy is an angel in Heaven, sweetheart. She's watching over Maisie every day, but we can't see her because we don't have magic eyes.

We can feel angels though, sometimes, if they're very near us. Or they might even leave us one of their feathers, like the ones on Maisie's angel dress for your nativity.'

Craig looked over at Clara, gratitude and relief evident on his face. *It's so nice to have someone to share things with,* he thought to himself.

'Yes,' said Maisie happily, clearly comforted by this explanation, 'she's always with me.'

The day was busy and fun-filled, with Father Christmas' Grotto, a Winter-Wonderland themed tree hut restaurant for lunch, hot chocolate by the rose garden, losing themselves in the maze and finally, the much-anticipated snowman parade. Craig could not remember when he had last had such a good time. Conversation flowed easily between him and Clara, and Maisie had been particularly taken with her, holding Clara's hand all day long. When Felix couldn't see the parade properly, Craig lifted him onto his shoulders so he could get the full effect of their clowning around. There were snowmen pulling others on sledges, some roller-skating, a chef, a snowman with a Christmas tree on his head, a baby snowman with his mum.... And Felix squealed and pointed at every one of them.

Maisie wasn't so interested in the parade, so Clara took her off to listen to Mrs Claus tell a Christmas story by the log fire in the craft hut. Craig and Felix met them there. As Felix recounted every character he'd seen, barely pausing for breath, Clara looked over his little head and straight at Craig. Their eyes locked and they shared a moment of mutual understanding. They both smiled. Craig had never seen Clara look so lovely as in that moment, with the fairy lights reflecting in her eyes, and her cheeks rosy from the chill outside. To be fair, he had never looked at her as he was now. Had never seen her as a woman and not just another parent from the school gates.

The children ran ahead, laughing as it started to snow lightly, landing in their hair and on their noses. The jumped up, trying to catch the flakes as they fell.

Craig and Clara laughed too, walking slowly behind in

companiable silence.

'I was wondering,' Craig began, then hesitated.

'Yes?' Clara quietly prompted him to continue.

'If perhaps you'd like to go out for a meal with me? Without the kids, I mean. In the holidays?' Craig couldn't believe what he was doing. He hadn't had a meal with any woman other than his mum since Marta had died. *Am I just doing this for Maisie?* he asked himself, relieved when his own heart answered a resounding 'No'. He looked at Clara, who in turn was looking at him from big brown eyes. He was certainly attracted to her, in every way, he decided.

'That would be lovely!' Clara replied without hesitation, linking her arm into his as they walked towards the car.

'Daddy, Daddy!' Maisie's shout had Craig sprinting the last few steps to the car.

'Look!' Nestled inside Maisie's lilac, knitted glove was a perfectly-formed, white feather. 'It was on the ground next to my door!' Maisie shouted excitedly. 'It's from my Mummy. Isn't it Miss Clara? That's what you said, wasn't it?'

'Yes, Maisie,' Clara said very gently, couching down to be at eye-level with the girl.

'It must be a message from your angel mummy, reminding you how much she loves you!' Clara held out both her arms and Maisie rushed into them, happy tears in her little eyes, and the feather clutched tightly in her palm.

The lump had returned to Craig's throat, only this time there was no swallowing it. He fussed about, getting Felix into his car seat, until tears no longer threatened. Clara and Maisie were still locked in an embrace, and Craig was moved to see that they were both crying. Unhindered, Clara's tears fell to mingle with Maisie's, until Maisie pulled away and said, 'That was lovely!' before jumping into the car, her precious feather still in hand.

'How quickly children bounce back,' Clara said, clearly embarrassed by her own emotions and trying desperately to get them back under control.

Without a second thought, Craig approached Clara and welcomed her into an embrace. She rested her head on his shoulder and he patted her back slowly, affectionately.

When they got into the car, Maisie piped up, 'I think you need to kiss Miss Clara better! Like you do with me!'

Clara looked at him, shaking her head slightly to indicate that he shouldn't feel obliged.

'It's not obligation,' Craig whispered, 'I'd like to.'

Clara smiled through watery eyes and nodded.

Craig leaned in and gave her a quick peck on the lips. Maisie giggled and Felix shouted, 'Yuck!'

Craig turned on the car engine and they listened to Christmas songs all the way home, singing along merrily.

When the busyness of the Big Day was over, presents all opened, too much eaten, and Santa Claus back in the North Pole till next year, Craig met Clara at a local bistro pub. She looked lovely, dressed in dark purple, with a sparkly silver clip in her hair. Craig opened the door for her and hoped he could hide his nerves.

He needn't have worried. They sat down at a table in the corner, next to the roaring log fire, and Clara admitted, 'I haven't done this since Felix was born, I'm sorry if nerves get the better of me!'

With that, Craig was able to admit his own jitters, and they settled into a comfortable conversation.

Neither was looking to rush into anything, and that suited them both just fine. As the fire crackled and the evening turned into night, Craig took Clara's hand across the table, and thanked his guardian angels – both of them – for bringing her into his life.

5. DECK THE SMALLS

Liv stood back and admired herself in the full-length mirror. She had definitely made the right choice, she decided, smiling at her reflection. The Mrs. Claus outfit was certainly one of their racier festive ensembles, but Liv had managed to make it work for her by wearing green leggings and a red tank top underneath. Her dad would have a fit if he saw her!

Stella, the owner of the lingerie boutique where Liv worked, who had declined to dress up herself, smiled at Liv and gave her a double thumbs-up from her spot behind the small counter where she was writing Christmas cards to their loyal customers.

The same Christmas mix had been on their ancient music player for the whole morning, but Liv didn't care. Christmas was her favourite time of year, and she loved everything about it, the cheesy tunes in particular!

Just then, the little bell above the door tinkled and a young guy walked in. Liv was startled. This was not their usual customer. Nevertheless, she smiled her most pleasant, welcoming expression and walked over to where he hovered beside a rack of Christmas pudding bras.

'Hello, Are you looking for anything in particular? For a special someone?' Liv asked. The bloke stood there, mouth agape, looking dumbfounded, and a bit like a guppy gasping for air. *He looks about the same age as me,* Liv thought, *though guys in their early twenties, in my experience, usually have more swagger than this.*

'Is it for your girlfriend?' She asked, deciding he must simply be frozen by embarrassment. *Poor thing.*

'NO!' he replied, rather too loudly to have been polite. 'Sorry, no, it's um… my mum.'

'You want to buy sexy lingerie for your mum?' Liv asked, about to put him in the 'pervert' box in her head.

'Aunt!' he exclaimed quickly.

Ok, make that the creepy pervert box, Liv decided.

Out loud, she simply said, 'Ah, so you want your mum and aunt to match?'

'No, no, no,' the man said, clearly trying to backtrack now that his sick fetish was out in the open. 'Can I start again?'

'Please, please do!' Liv welcomed.

'So,' he began, letting out a long breath, and muttering *I'm no good at this* to himself.

'My name is Daniel. Dan. I've seen you here a few times through the window. I work in the coffee shop around the corner. You've been in a few times, too.'

'Yesss…' Liv said, hoping a point would be reached soon…

'And I wondered if you'd like…?' he tailed off.

'Some lingerie?' Liv asked, raising her eyebrow.

'No, well I mean you look great, wow, but no. I was wondering if you'd go out for a drink with me?' Dan turned beetroot and shuffled backwards, banging into a mannequin dressed only in a see-through, silvery basque, adorned with sequin snowflakes.

'Ahhh,' he said, and lurched forward again.

Liv smiled awkwardly, not sure what to say. I mean, he's cute, she thought, taking in the dishevelled hair and wonky glasses. Kind of a mad professor look he's got going on there.

Her social calendar was sadly empty since coming home from a gap year in Japan after university, so Liv decided to take a chance and said, 'Thanks, that would be nice.'

Poor Dan looked so shocked, she thought she might have to give him one of the candy canes from the tree in the window, just to bring his blood sugar back up again.

'P-Perfect,' he stammered, turning round and exiting through the door he had only just entered.

Two seconds later, he was back, looking redder than ever.

'I'd best get your number.'

'Of course,' Liv said, trying to stifle a giggle.

Friday of that same week, the pair found themselves sitting in the local pub, fire roaring, Christmas tunes playing, and the barman wearing a silly Santa's Helper hat.

Liv stared at her rum and coke, wondering if she'd made a mistake by accepting Dan's invitation. He himself sat tapping his fingers nervously on the side of his pint glass, face red from the fire. He seemed to be wearing contact lenses today, as the cute glasses had disappeared. She could see his eyes more clearly, though. They were mesmerizing – brown around the edges and green flecked with amber in the middle. He saw her looking at him intently and smiled awkwardly.

'Have you had a good week?' Liv asked, hoping to initiate conversation.

'Just the coffee shop,' he said, 'they've got us wearing festive T-shirts. It's not really my thing.'

'Oh?' Liv prompted him to continue, 'What is your thing then?'

'Well,' he began hesitantly, 'it's photography actually! I love the process of it. I'm doing a course at the local college....'

And with that he was off, relaxing into a subject he felt comfortable with. Liv smiled, nodding and making appropriate responses.

Another round of drinks and a bowl of chips later, they walked out into the freezing air. Liv blew out and watched her breath rise up and away. She took Dan's hand as they walked through the park in the centre of town. He seemed a bit surprised at first, but didn't pull away. In fact, she could feel him squeezing her hand intermittently as if wanting to reassure himself that she was really still there. Their conversation flowed easily now after the rocky start in the pub, and they chatted away happily, watching a flock of geese fly overhead, their happy honking loud and incessant.

Liv stood and watched them form the perfect V-shape, before looking sideways at Dan. He was staring at her intently, and she turned so that she faced him fully.

'You really are stunning, you know?' Dan said, the first time she had heard him start a conversation without stammering in hesitation.

'Well, thank you, but, I mean I...'

'Shhh,' Dan said, leaning down to kiss her. He didn't have to lean far, as Liv was tall for a girl – almost six feet. At six foot two, Dan was only slightly taller. Their lips didn't quite meet before they bumped noses. Liv laughed, and rubbed her nose against Dan's in an eskimo-style kiss. She didn't want him to lose his bottle!

A slight re-adjustment and they locked together perfectly. Their cold breath mingling, holding hands tightly, unaware of their surroundings.

They were interrupted a short moment later by the sound of screeching wheels and a little voice saying, 'Uncle Dan, UNCLE DAN! Get off that girl!'

They moved apart, embarrassed, to see a little boy of about six pulling on Dan's sleeve. A woman running towards them was shouting 'Sam! Sam! Wait! Too Fast!'

Sam's scooter had been discarded and he was jumping up and down next to Dan.

'We saw Santa!' he shouted, 'in his grotto, over there!!'

'Wow, wow, that's great,' Dan said, shooting apologetic glances at Liv. Liv herself had no siblings, and very little experience with small people. She simply stood there, freezing and bemused.

'Who's this?' the boy asked, looking Liv up and down and clearly not rating her much.

'This is, ah, Liv,' Dan stammered.

'Is she your girlfriend?'

'Sammy! Stop interrogating your uncle. It's like twenty questions with you today! Poor Santa was glad to get back to his reindeer, I'm sure! Hi little brother!'

The woman affectionately rubbed Dan's arm, turning to Liv and saying, 'Hi, I'm Emma!'

'Hi!' Liv said. Now it was her turn to shift awkwardly from foot to foot. Both Liv's mum and Dad were quiet, academic types, and didn't go in for loud family times. Liv was totally out of her element. 'I'd better be going,' she said, flashing a weak smile at Dan.

'No, no,' Emma insisted, 'Please don't go on our account, we're heading home to get this scooter speedster into the bath.'

She kissed Dan's check and dragged Sam away, the little boy clearly reluctant to leave his favourite uncle.

'Sorry,' Dan said, taking her hand again. But the moment has passed, and dusk was drawing in making the air even icier.

'I have to get back,' Liv said, 'I'm helping my mum make Christingles for the church.'

'Ok, ok,' Dan said, 'Let me walk you.'

They walked arm in arm out the other side of the park, and only a few streets away where Liv lived in a tall, modern townhouse with her parents.

'I'd ask you in,' she said sadly, 'but they're not keen on unexpected visitors. They like things planned in advance, you know...'

'Sure,' Dan said, trying to understand. His family were the complete opposite. With five brothers and two sisters coming and going, his parents' house was always too busy to stand on ceremony.

'Listen,' he said, trying to eek their time out further and maybe even get to see her again, 'Why don't we go out for hot chocolate on Sunday, and then to the outdoor ice rink in Mayor's Square?'

Liv liked that idea. She liked Dan. She relaxed and flashed him her best smile, 'Perfect.'

'I'm working till one,' Dan continued, 'perhaps you could meet me at the coffee shop then?'

'Definitely,' Liv said, giving him a look that clearly invited another kiss. Dan didn't need to be asked twice and kissed her with a passion which surprised her. *Not so shy now!* Liv thought to herself contentedly, responding in kind. They stood there, in the middle of her driveway, locked in an embrace that heated them both from the tips of their frozen toes to the top of their woolly hats.

Liv worked in the shop all day Saturday. It was amazing how many men came in to buy Christmas-themed sets for their wives (Not all for their wives, Liv concluded, especially the guy who had told her he was paying in cash so that it wouldn't show up on his bank statement. *Horrible little man,* Liv thought).

Just before closing, the door chimed and a tall man strode in. *No sneaking in guiltily for this guy,* Liv noted, slightly impressed. He started looking through the rails confidently.

'Can I help you find something in particular?' Liv asked, walking over to their 'exclusive' range where he was standing.

('Exclusive basically means barely there,' Stella had told her when the stock came in last month.)

'Yes, thank you,' the guy said, pointing to a black and gold sheer set with beautiful, embroidered stars in appropriate, modesty-covering places, 'Do you have this in a size twelve?'

'I'll just check for you, Sir!' Liv walked away to the little storeroom at the back of the shop. She had a strange feeling, like she'd met the man before. He seemed familiar. *He must be a regular,* Liv thought, *he certainly knows what he wants.*

All wrapped in tissue paper, with a shiny red bow and gift bag to match, the bloke went happily on his way, and Liv thought no more about him. Her feet were aching, and she couldn't wait for a long soak. One day closer to seeing Dan, she smiled happily to herself.

Sunday arrived with frost on the ground and a nip in the air. Liv dressed up warmly in black jeggings and a Christmas jumper with a cute reindeer on it. The reindeer's nose was an actual pompom attached to the front, which lit up when you squeezed it. She arrived at the coffee shop just before one and waved to Dan through the window. He was wearing a 'Ho Ho Hot Coffee' T-shirt with a picture of a large Santa's head emblazoned across the front.

Dan beckoned Liv to enter, and she walked up to the counter.

'Hi!' he said cheerfully, 'I'll be right with you. Would you like a drink?'

'Sure,' Liv said, I'll have a white, hot chocolate mocha, with extra marshmallows and chocolate snowflakes, please!'

Dan smiled a wide smile, 'How did I know you'd have something so sweet?' he teased.

An hour later they were on the ice rink, equipped with gloves, scarves and hats, and still freezing cold! When he'd made the invitation, Liv had assumed that Dan could skate. Nope, not at all! What he lacked in ability, though, he made up for in enthusiasm, and they laughed their way around the ice with him clinging onto her arm, his legs flailing in every direction like a baby giraffe.

'I haven't laughed that much in ages!' Liv exclaimed as they took a much-needed breather by the side.

'Me neither!' Dan agreed, rubbing his knees which had certainly taken a battering in several falls.

When he stood up fully straight again, Liv wasted no time in unzipping Dan's winter coat slightly and putting her hands inside to warm them up on his sweater. Leaning into him, she looked up as he leaned down and kissed her. First, he pecked her cold, rosy nose, warming it up from numb. Then he peppered kisses around her forehead and across her cheekbones, making Liv giggle from their feathery tickle. It was lovely, but Liv needed the good stuff. She caught his lips on their second pass around, and kissed him hungrily, rubbing her hands against his chest. Dan had his arms wrapped around her torso, and they stood there locked together until a group of teenagers skated past, wolf whistling and shouting 'Oy, Get a room!'

Dan pulled away, embarrassed, but Liv simply stuck her tongue out at their retreating backs and found Dan's lips again.

When they paused, Dan looked at her seriously, intently, from those gorgeous eyes that Liv could so easily get lost in, and asked her nervously, 'Liv, will you go out with me?'

'We are out!' she said, deliberately missing the point.

Seeing his dejected, little-boy look, Liv took pity on him, 'Of course I'll go out with you, silly! You're already my boyfriend!'

Dan relaxed again instantly, hugging her closer and kissing the top of her hair. 'Wow, I'm so lucky, Liv!'

'And don't you forget it!' she teased.

A week later was Christmas Eve, and Liv was relaxing on her sofa with Dan. Her parents had gone carol singing with some friends of theirs from church, and Liv and Dan were making the most of having the house to themselves. Christmas music blaring, Quality Street opened, and a Christmas movie that neither of them were paying attention to. Stella had given Liv a Christmas bonus and offered her some of the remaining festive lingerie. She had chosen a very modest red shorts and crop top set, with dancing snowmen around the edges. Dan seemed to approve heartily of her choice and enjoyed following the snowmen with kisses. *He's so sweet*, Liv thought to herself, her heart full. No pressure, no rush, just sweet time together.

The pair were both disappointed when Dan had to leave at tea-time to go for a huge holiday meal with his family. Liv had been invited, but wasn't yet ready to face the whole clan, especially at such a crazy time of year. Dan had understood completely, reassuring her that he didn't mind.

'You could come round on Boxing Day, though,' he suggested hopefully, 'there'll only be me and one sister there by then.'

'Okay,' Liv agreed, wondering how she'd manage a whole day without seeing him.

Christmas Day came and went, with text messages between them pinging in several times an hour, and a long WhatsApp video call in the evening.

At ten in the morning on Boxing Day Liv arrived at Dan's house, a large Victorian terraced building with a huge wreath on the welcoming porch. She rang the bell nervously and heard a basic rendition of 'Deck the Halls' chiming clunkily in the hall.

The door was swiftly opened, and Liv looked open-mouthed at the man in front of her. She was frozen to the spot, and not from cold this time. It was no other than the tall customer from the lingerie shop.

'It's for me!' Dan said, pushing his dad out of the way, and ushering Liv in out of the cold.

Liv certainly felt chilled. She was unsure whether she should acknowledge having met Dan's dad before, or just pretend otherwise. After all, she had no reason to believe the set hadn't been for Dan's mum. Still, it was all very embarrassing.

She needn't have worried. 'We've already met!' Shaun exclaimed as Dan introduced them, 'You're the little elf from the smalls shop!'

'Yes, yes I am,' Liv admitted, relieved.

'Oh Shaun, you didn't go to Liv's shop to get my annual set. Did you?' Dan's mum asked, laughing and pushing her husband's arm cheekily.

'Well, I didn't know it was Dan's girlfriend's shop, did I?' Shaun said, laughing along with her.

Liv relaxed, smiling back at them both.

'Let's get out of here!' Dan whispered in her ear, taking Liv's hand and leading her up the brightly decorated staircase. 'What festive treat have you got on from Stella's shop today?' he asked, a twinkle in his eye and a promising smile on his face. Liv couldn't wait to show him.

6. MEG AND MAX

Meg sat on the cold, hard sand, the freezing waves lapping at her toes. It was winter in Scotland, but Meg didn't care. She found the movement of the waves against her bare feet a form of therapy. Wrapped up in her padded coat, with her flask of coffee resting beside her, Meg reached inside her voluminous handbag for her journal.

West Sands, being the spot where 'Chariots of Fire' filmed its famous beach race, was normally a tourist hotspot in St Andrews, but today it was deserted. The students had evacuated the town to head home for Christmas, the local folk were busy at work and home preparing for the festive season, and the beach was not so inviting at this time of year.

Meg had finished her work for the morning. She had graduated from the university in the town three years before but, to her mother's extreme chagrin, had decided to stay on and tutor French to high school students. This didn't quite pay her bills, however, so Meg also worked in Inveraray of Scotland, a local tartan and souvenir shop. This time of day in the early afternoon, between her shopwork and her tutoring, was Meg's time for herself. Most days she could be found here, scribbling away in her floral notebook or simply looking out to sea.

On this particular day, Meg's nerves were in shreds. She had dealt with a particularly impatient customer, who was angry that their woollen scarves had not come into stock yet. They had ranted for several minutes as 'they urgently needed to post them overseas for Christmas.' Meg had done her best to placate, but apparently nothing can soothe the wrath of the last-minute Christmas shopper who cannot get their hands on their chosen item immediately.

As was usual on this beach, at this time of year, a strong wind was blowing sideways across the sand, forcing Meg to pull her hood over her ears and cling onto her pages. For this reason, she didn't hear her new companion until they jumped on her from behind, sending Meg flying, face-first towards the waves. Her journal flew one way, her pen the other, and Meg caught herself on her hands, her forearms flat in the waves.

'What the...?' Meg asked into the air, almost too afraid to turn around. From the corner of her eye she saw a huge, shaggy beast coming up to her face.

'Arrgghh!' Meg shouted and jumped up as fast as she could. She had never been an animal lover. But animals with no sense of space? Those were her pet hate.

Two extremely pointed ears, a furry black face, and a huge brown, hairy body which came up to her knees were enough to have Meg backing off slowly, her belongings forgotten in the sand.

The canine, however, seemed very agitated and followed her quickly, swaying its tail forcefully, its eyes focused on Meg. She looked around for an owner, or anybody really, to save her, but none were visible.

The dog darted forward. Meg screamed and froze. Rushing behind her, the beast pushed its snout into the crook behind Meg's knee, propelling her forward. Try as she might, Meg could not get away from it and, in the end, she allowed herself to be pushed forwards in the direction of the sand dunes which lined the back of the two-mile-long beach.

Not one given to swearing, Meg thought of a few choice words which she would happily have shouted at that moment. Instead, tears formed in her eyes, partly from the icy wind and partly from her predicament.

As they neared the dunes, a flash of fluorescent yellow caught Meg's eye. The dog behind her stopped prodding and began barking – low, urgent sounds that encouraged Meg to walk on and investigate.

There, mostly hidden in the grass between two large sand dunes was a man. He had clearly been running or doing exercise of some sort, judging by his bright Lycra attire. Meg rushed forwards, of her own volition this time, and kneeled down beside the stranger. She checked his pulse, definitely still breathing. *Thank goodness!*

Feeling her hand on his arm, the man came around long enough to point feebly to his neck. A thin chain held a dog tag, which indicated that he was diabetic. Meg realised that she recognised the guy from around town – one of the quirks of living in a small place was that you often saw the same people over and over as the months went by. She remembered having spoken to him a few times in the queue of her favourite coffee shop. He had been friendly and chatty.

'Ok, ok, let's not panic,' Meg said, mostly to herself, 'let's get you some help, you'll be fine.' She removed her padded coat and put it over him to keep him warm. Meg didn't have any first aid training (though that was certainly top of her self-investment list for the New Year after this!), but she'd had a friend at university who had diabetes, and Meg remembered that chocolate was important. Embarrassed to her core, but feeling it was necessary, she quickly patted down the man's tight clothing for hidden pockets. Neither sweet treats nor any form of injectable medicine was found.

The dog, who had started whimpering and pacing in circles, nudged Meg from time to time.

'Ok, ok,' she tried to reassure the animal as she searched in her jeans pocket for her mobile phone. Meg dialled the emergency services and spoke to the operator, explaining that she'd found an unconscious man who was diabetic. They assured her that an ambulance had been dispatched immediately. The road running along the back of the beach separating the dunes from the golf courses and clubhouse behind was more of a track, and Meg could see no distinguishing features to direct the paramedics to her exact spot. In a flash of inspiration, she took the animal by the collar.

'Okay,' she said trying to sound confident, whilst thinking, *Dogs can sense fear, please be kind to me!* Meg looked at the tag attached to the reflective material of the collar.

Max.

'Okay, that's great, that's great, Max I'm Meg, I need you to do a job for me.'

Max was initially very reluctant to be led away from his owner. He kept looking over his shoulder and whining as Meg led him the small distance to the grassed area by the tarmacked track. Meg continued speaking in calm, reassuring whispers, before finally saying, with as much courage and command as she could muster, 'STAY!'

Without looking back, Meg ran back to her patient. He had not moved but thankfully was still breathing regularly. His body was sweating and shaking slightly. Meg was not sure whether to remove her coat or not, but in the end decided to leave it blanketing him.

It felt like an age until Meg heard the distinctive sirens in the distance, when in fact it had only been eight minutes. St Andrews didn't possess a proper A&E, instead having only a small cottage hospital. Yet, here they came, and Meg could not have been more relieved. She heard the engine stop and voices as two men rushed through the dunes with Max running ahead to guide them.

'I found him like this!' Meg blurted, 'he has nothing on him. I didn't know what to do. Will he be ok?'

'Aye, let us in to see now, lassie,' one of the paramedics said gruffly, kneeling down.

Meg was more than happy to comply. Hovering nearby with Max, she felt him nuzzle her leg and absentmindedly reached down to stroke the top of his head. He licked her palm appreciatively, and for once Meg didn't recoil.

Watching the paramedic give the stranger an injection, Meg wondered if she should leave. She had just remembered her handbag and boots still sitting on the sand.

'He's going to come around shortly,' the second paramedic said, coming up beside her, 'Probably a hypo, but he'll need the once-over at the hospital.'

Meg nodded, the full implication of his meaning not hitting her until the man continued, 'so you'll be needing to keep his pet with ye.'

You what now?

'Um, I'm not sure that'll be possible,' Meg replied, a sinking feeling filling her.

'Aye well, he cannae be coming into the ambulance, now can he?' he chuckled.

'No, I guess not.' Meg had no idea how she would manage this.

She saw the lead lying in the sand, and picked it up, before hesitantly attaching it to Max's collar. Max appeared calm now that his human was being looked after and had lain down beside Meg.

'Lovely animal that,' the paramedic mused, 'Me Granda used to have a German shepherd, not wi' the long hair, mind, a lot o' bother all that brushing!'

Meg nodded silently.

A few minutes later, she and Max watched as the two men loaded their patient into the ambulance and drove away, sirens blaring once more. Luckily, Meg had remembered at the last minute to scribble her contact details on their notes. She didn't want to be left with Max for a minute longer than was necessary!

Meg and Max took their time walking back to her abandoned belongings, her notepad was wet beyond repair, but everything else seemed fine. Other than the wind, the day was still bright and clear. Praying that Max would have no toilet breaks along the road, as she was woefully unprepared for that, Meg made her way back along The Scores, seeing the fancy hotels dressed for the Christmas season, along past the ancient castle, and down the small hill towards the harbour where she rented a tiny studio flat.

'How's this going to work then, Max?' Meg asked the dog, wondering if he would allow himself to be led inside a strange building.

Thankfully, he came happily along the tiny corridor with her, and waited patiently as Meg unlocked her front door. 'Shush now,' she had warned him, as strictly speaking animals were against the terms of her lease.

Finding Max a bowl of water and some roast chicken that she had been saving to put in a salad that evening, Meg quickly set up her laptop for her first tutorial of the day, which was via Zoom.

A few hours passed and Meg and Max were cosy on the sofa when the doorbell rang. Max immediately began barking, protectively, and Meg smiled at him, 'Good dog, good dog, stay!' She was definitely warming to him, and the company he provided, as reluctant as Meg herself was to admit it.

Meg opened the door to find the man from the beach, looking

much more alive, though very pale.

'We met at the beach,' he said, 'Well, we didn't actually meet. I'm so sorry if I gave you a fright, finding me like that. I shouldn't have skipped lunch and then gone for a run. Thank you so much for everything you did.'

Hearing his master's voice, Max come bounding down the hallway, almost knocking Meg off her feet again.

'Sorry, sorry,' the stranger apologised repeatedly, as he himself was covered in slobbery dog kisses.

'Um, would you like to come in?' Meg asked, more out of politeness than a desire to converse further.

'No thanks, I still feel groggy and tired. Bed for me, I think!'

Meg relaxed as she waved goodbye to the pair and headed inside for a well-earned rest.

Ten minutes later her phone buzzed.

Jack here again. Man from the beach, sorry never introduced myself. Early dinner tomorrow to say thank you?

Meg didn't normally accept invites from strange men. *Well, to be honest, this was her first, but she should have that as a rule, surely?*

That being said, was he really a stranger? Meg wondered. After going to and fro in her mind, she decided to take a chance.

She hadn't dated since the year before last, when an unfortunate Tinder match had left her happy to remain in her own company for a long time to come. Yes, her one and only foray into online dating had ended with Meg being screamed at in the store where she worked, 'Flower of Scotland' playing merrily in the background, as an upset wife berated her for having dinner with her husband. The fact that it had literally only been a bag of chips and a can of Iron Bru (last of the big spenders, that one) and Meg had vehemently declined his offer of 'showing her a right good time,' had not been communicated to the poor woman. Add to that the fact that he'd conveniently failed to mention his wife to Meg in their two weeks of texting before the date, and both women had apparently been left in the dark. Meg had stood, shocked, until her boss had ushered the screaming banshee out, telling her to take it up with her errant husband. Yes, it had been enough to put Meg off dating indefinitely.

Anyway, onwards and upwards! Thought Meg hopefully, assessing the contents of her meagre wardrobe. Aside from the delightfully itchy plaid skirt she had to wear for work, Meg had surprisingly little to wear that could actually be classed as feminine. In the end, she opted for black trousers and a black polo neck jumper. *(Well, it was winter after all!)*

They had agreed to meet at the end of South Street, beside the old archway. There were a lot of pubs and restaurants around there, and they'd decided to choose their venue together. As she approached, Meg was surprised to see that Jack had brought Max with him. The pair looked very cute, though, with Max wearing a green bow tie around his furry neck, and Jack in a shirt of the same colour. Jack's dirty-blond hair and bright eyes were set off perfectly by his choice, and Meg flashed a genuine smile as she neared them.

Spotting his new favourite buddy, Max lurched forwards, pulling the lead out of Jack's hand, and stood on his back paws to reach Meg's face.

'Urrgghhmm,' she spluttered through a mouthful of fur and dog kisses.

'I am so sorry,' Jack apologised, as he struggled to pull Max back, 'I guess he really likes you!'

'No kidding!' Meg exclaimed, wiping her face on the tissue he offered.

'There are a lot of dog friendly places around here,' Jack said, by way of explanation.

Ensconced in a cosy corner of the Homely Hound (*How apt!* Meg thought), they enjoyed a lovely meal and chatted about what had brought them to, and kept them in, this quaint Scottish town.

Jack explained that he was a research scientist, studying for a PhD in Molecular Biology. 'I'm in my final year,' he added, 'but I'm hoping to stay on to do some paid research in the lab,' he gave her a pointed, hopeful look at this point, and Meg smiled nervously. She wasn't sure she was ready to jump into anything so fast.

They had a great evening, walking up to the grassy cathedral ruins after their meal, where Max enjoyed sniffing around and galloping along after them. They stopped under a large tree, where someone had thoughtfully tied a large twig of mistletoe to the nearest branch. Pausing in the twilight, Jack turned to Meg and said, 'Thank you again for yesterday. Really. Without you, I don't know what would have happened.'

'It was all Max, really,' replied Meg modestly, transfixed by the light flickering in his eyes. Originally a hazel brown, they had now become dark and stormy, like the waves crashing nearby.

As if attached to him by an invisible string, Meg leaned towards Jack, as he brought his lips down on hers. Gently, to begin, and then with a growing sense of urgency. Meg felt as if she was floating above the ground, light as air.

'I'd love to see you again,' Jack ventured as they stood outside Meg's apartment block, 'if you'd like?'

One pair of big, earnest eyes would have been enough to convince her, but since Meg had two sets staring at her hopefully, how could she refuse? Not that she'd really wanted to. After all, it's not often that you rescue your own Christmas wish-come-true.

7. ALASKAN ADVENT-URE

Finn sighed heavily as he shrugged out of his snowsuit. The icy blast that was following him in from the open door made him shiver, and he reached out his leg to slam it closed. The trip into Anchorage for Christmas gifts had done little to improve his foul temper. In two days' time, he would be leaving the Chugach Research Centre, which had been his base in the state park for the last nine months, and returning home to Ireland to spend Christmas with his family.

The thought should have filled Finn with pleasure, as he had certainly missed the whole crazy lot of them, yet the closer the day came, the more his mood worsened.

The cause of his bad-tempered demeanour, Finn knew, was sitting in the common room next door – all five foot six of her, with fiery red hair and beautiful green eyes, and a mouth that was made for kissing.

Shannon. He had fallen for her on the plane over here and fallen hard. She was the only other scientist from Ireland, but that wasn't the reason for his longing. No, the cause was partly his huge physical attraction to her (which, try as he might, Finn could not switch off), and also her quick, sassy attitude and no-nonsense approach. She was the full package.

Shame, then, that she couldn't bear to be in the same room as him for more than ten seconds.

Finn left his outdoor gear over the rack to dry and headed into the lounge. Over half of his colleagues had already headed back to wherever in the world they hailed from. As soon as the last expedition of the year was complete, the data input and paperwork done and dusted, they had said their goodbyes and disappeared almost overnight. Finn could have gone with them, of course, but he had hung around, making excuses such as needing to check his student groupings for the teams arriving in February, and working on the journal paper he was writing on wilderness survival skills.

Looking up from her laptop as Finn entered the room, Shannon sighed inwardly. She wasn't sure she could keep up this disinterested attitude much longer. He was gorgeous – cute, funny, intelligent, saw her as an equal, and had a fantastic six-pack to boot – but she had promised herself not to have another relationship with a colleague, and she was determined to stick to that plan. As much as her body hated her for it.

She could see the way he looked at her, when he thought she was engrossed in a task. That piercing gaze, as if he could see straight into her heart, always gave her a pleasant shiver of awareness. But no, back home in Ireland, Stu had put her off workplace dating for life – once bitten twice shy, and all that.

It had gotten to the point, though, that she had to leave a room whenever Finn entered it, so little could she trust her own responses. Her heightened awareness of him must surely be plain to see, so she opted for the safest option – running away from the problem.

Finn saw Shannon begin to close her laptop, and the anger began to rise in him again. He really wanted to know why she disliked him so much. *Surely, he couldn't have annoyed her so badly?*

He didn't recall any huge faux pas. Of course, there had been that end of expedition party a few months ago, which had seen many of his colleagues (he included) sharing one too many shots of bourbon. And he did recall slurring, telling the guys in no uncertain terms that he thought she was as hot as…. Well, he was sure she hadn't heard. Besides, Shannon had been avoiding him for months before that. He decided that he wouldn't go a day longer without having it out with her. He had a right to know why she had side-lined him.

As Shannon stood up, she had the awareness that he was right behind the sofa. She turned slowly, her skin tingled and her stomach lurched in awareness of his proximity. She looked at Finn questioningly. *Surely he must have got the message by now?* she hoped. Shannon didn't have the willpower to resist if he came on to her.

'H-Hi!' Finn stuttered, his mouth suddenly as dry as a riverbed in a drought, 'Since we're the only ones about, I thought you might like to chat?' he wasn't convincing, even to his own ears, and shrugged his shoulders by way of emphasising his point.

'About what?' Shannon asked, her green eyes flashing mischievously.

About the weather, what do you think? Finn kept his sarcasm to himself. Although the old, tattered sofa separated them, he was close enough to smell her rosewater perfume and it was driving him mad.

'About our plans for the holidays? Are you looking forward to getting back to Cork?'

'Of course, it's been a long, cold time away!' Shannon replied, her reference to temperature making Finn want to heat her right up, the way she was doing to him.

Shannon looked at him expectantly, waiting for more conversation to follow, but he had nothing. He could barely think straight.

'Well, I better be getting on,' she said eventually, 'I have most of my packing still to do.'

'WAIT!' Finn shouted, startling them both, 'sorry, that came out louder than I expected!' *I'm sounding like a total prat!*

Shannon stood, frozen to the spot. Her body hoped he was about to name the chemistry between them, to give it life so that they could both acknowledge it, while her head knew she needed to beat a hasty retreat.

'Perhaps we could have a beer in the snug after dinner?'

'Um, sure, ok,' the words were out of her mouth before her brain had a chance to concoct an excuse. Shannon hurried off, leaving Finn feeling like another freezing cold walk outside was in order to cool his raging senses.

Dinner was a meagre affair, since the chefs who had been hired to provide catering had left after the last paying group. Providing training in earth sciences, wilderness survival, team building and mountaineering skills, the scientists hosted cohorts of students every couple of months. It paid the bills for the research centre and allowed the team to continue their own scientific projects in glaciology, geology, climatology and biology – their expeditions often taking them to all corners of the state. With everything winding down till the New Year, however, they were now eating frozen ready meals and spending the evenings by the log fire in the tiny snug which was reserved for permanent team members only.

Shannon managed to avoid eating with Finn, having decided to complete nearly all of her packing instead. It was quite late when she entered the snug, hoping to find all of her remaining colleagues there. To her dismay, only Finn sat alone by the fire, his feet up on a stool and his headphones over his ears.

Perhaps if I sneak back out, he won't know I was here? Shannon wondered, hoped even.

The tiny hairs on the back of Finn's neck alerted him to her presence. He turned quickly to see her hovering in the doorway, like a rabbit caught in the headlights. He tried to rip his headphones off in a hurry, and failed miserably, getting the wires tangled around his neck. *Why do I always look like a clown in front of her?* Finn lamented silently.

Shannon mustered what little confidence she could, and walked into the room, deliberately sitting on the far sofa. The room being so small, however, it was still way too close to Finn for her liking.

'I got my packing done,' she said, by way of breaking the ice between them.

'Good, yes, great,' he said, not knowing how else to respond. Suddenly sick of the ridiculous exchange of pleasantries which was the recipe for every stilted conversation between them, Finn exclaimed, 'Why do you constantly avoid me? What have I done to upset you?'

He realised he sounded like a whiny teenager, and at that point didn't even care.

Shannon sat, fiddling with her long hair uncomfortably, 'Well, I, I mean, nothing. You've done nothing,' she blurted, hoping that would satisfy him, but knowing that he'd probably just ripped the lid off Pandora's box.

'Then why?' he asked, his blue eyes flashing a stormy grey.

'Because, well, because I don't want to end up in bed with you.'

'Bed? Excuse me?' Finn asked, not sure whether he'd interpreted her remark correctly. His body had reacted, that's for sure, but he couldn't quite get his head around her admission.

'I mean,' Shannon continued, quietly, 'I can't let my attraction to you take me somewhere which would end in an awkward disaster, so to speak!'

'Attraction?' Finn was aware that he was sounding ridiculous, parroting everything she said, and she was probably wondering how he ever managed to achieve a PhD in anything other than being an idiot.

'Yes,' Shannon replied firmly, trying to make it clear that she had no more to say on the subject.

Finn persevered, though, like a dog with a bone, 'So, you're attracted to me, and goodness knows I'm attracted to you, yet we can't spend more than five minutes together in case...'

'Yes, exactly,' Shannon finished for him, not wanting him to verbalise what might happen next.

She stood up, abruptly, seeking an escape. Finn was too quick for her this time, however, and jumped up and into her flight path before she could make it to the door.

'Please!' he shouted, 'Please, don't rush off,' he added more calmly, trying to rein in his confused emotions.

'I can't,' Shannon said, standing her ground, her eyes flashing like emeralds with arousal and anger, 'I've been down that road before, in the lab where I worked back home, and it was one of the reasons I ended up coming across the Atlantic to get away!'

'Okay, okay,' Finn whispered, trying to coax her into remaining in the room and give himself time to get things straight in his head, 'thank you, for sharing I mean, I understand. But what if it didn't turn out like that? What if we were great together? Couldn't you take a chance?'

Shannon could feel her resistance falling as his words breached the crumbling barrier of her willpower.

'Maybe,' she whispered, edging closer to where he stood.

Their eyes locked, storm crashing into fire, and their bodies quickly followed. It was like two magnets, inexplicably attracted to each other by a force so strong it couldn't be denied any longer.

There was no sweet slowness, no tentative exploration, just a powerful merging of mouths and bodies, hands exploring, no words needed.

Realising they were about to commit a very private act in a public place, Shannon pulled away. Every nerve ending, every sense she had was screaming at her to resume their passionate encounter, but she held her arms firmly down by her sides, her body quivering with the effort it took her. Seeing Finn about to take her in his arms again, Shannon put her hand against his chest in gentle restraint.

'Finn,' she said breathlessly, 'I know how much we both want this, believe me I do!' she took a deep breath before she was able to continue, 'but I don't want to rush into something so physical, so irreversible. I need us to slow things down a bit. Please.'

Finn took several deep breaths. He wasn't angry at all, he just needed a moment to control his raging... hormones.

'Of course,' he said, taking her hand, feeling the spark of electricity between them as he did so, 'but we can get to know each other, right? We can enjoy getting to know each other? Just a bit more slowly?'

Shannon flashed him a grin, the need in his voice turning her on more than he could have realised.

'Of course,' she reassured, taking hold of his other hand and closing the space between them, 'of course, we can get to know each other and... see where it leads us. In time, that's all, let's take our time!' With that she leaned in and brushed her lips against his. The fire ignited immediately and things became heated again.

When they pulled apart once more, Finn commented sarcastically, 'I hope it's snowing back in Ireland, too, I think I'm going to be taking a lot of cold walks these holidays!'

Shannon winked at him in reply, 'You certainly are Dr O'Sullivan, you certainly are!' and with that she captured his mouth once more.

8. ONE LAST PUSH

Darcy's patience had run out. Every last shred of it. If she didn't get this grocery shopping through the till and into her car without one more person asking her 'When are you due?' she would surely explode.

To be fair, though, the horror on their faces when she replied, 'This time LAST week!' was a slight comfort. Clearly, they then expected her waters to break right then and there! It was a very useful conversation stopper.

The incessant Christmas music in the supermarket, the crowds and the rush to grab everything vaguely seasonal from the shelves, had grated on Darcy since the moment she entered the shop.

Never mind, she kept telling herself, *I'm almost at the front of the queue.*

She needed to rush home and fix dinner for Joel. For the first time that week, he'd said she could expect him home at the normal time. Well, what used to be normal time. In the past few months, he had begun coming home later and later. At first, it was just every Wednesday evening working late, then, as the weeks progressed, he had added in another evening until this past fortnight had been ridiculous. Back aching and feet swollen every day, Darcy had often retired to bed before he came in, leaving his meal shrivelled and cold on the side to be re-heated.

'Hello, dear,' the friendly checkout assistant smiled and looked straight at Darcy's enormous bump. *Why did no-one look at her face anymore?* She knew what was coming before it had even left the woman's mouth,

'Ooh, you look far along. When are you due?'

'Overdue, actually,' Darcy stated, matter-of-factly, trying not to be rude. People were only interested, after all. 'My due date was last Thursday!'

'Oh you poor thing!' the lady exclaimed, 'you shouldn't be out shopping in your state!'

Darcy didn't like to explain that she had no option. Her family all lived out of the area and weren't due to arrive until her precious delivery had made an appearance. Since it was Christmas Eve in three days' time, and she and Joel still needed to eat…

Darcy was brought back to the moment, by a loud message on the tannoy system interrupting the dulcet tones of Frank Sinatra singing, 'Have yourself a Merry Little Christmas',

Help on aisle 9, that's help on aisle 9 please! And bring a chair!

Horrified, Darcy realised that the assistant in front of her was speaking into her microphone, and the requested aid was for herself!

'No, no, that's really not necessary,' Darcy pleaded, not wanting to be the centre of attention. Too late, a young lad who she'd earlier seen stacking shelves with bottles of sherry, appeared like lightening, clearly glad of the opportunity to change roles for a while.

'Carl, help this lady to pack please and then out to her car!'

The instruction given, Darcy accepted graciously. Well, as graciously as her screaming bladder allowed. She'd been here for too long and was starting to feel the effects. She sat down dejectedly in the offered plastic chair.

Once her shopping had been loaded in the boot, Darcy thanked Carl. She had no cash on her, so she'd given him a large satsuma for his trouble, to which the poor lad had looked slightly perplexed! Nevertheless, he'd thanked her politely for the token!

Darcy wedged herself behind the steering wheel, wondering how much longer she'd actually fit in this space. The need to go to the toilet was almost overwhelming now, and her back pain had increased significantly.

She had only travelled out of the supermarket, and onto the nearby dual carriageway, when the pain hit her. It started like one of Darcy's normal cramps at first. The midwife had told her it was Braxton Hicks contractions, just her body getting prepared for the birth. This one had started out like that, but the pain was more like a band across the top of her bump now, intense and demanding her attention.

Darcy pulled over in the next layby to breathe through the pain, the way she had been taught in their antenatal classes. Thankfully, as the group met on the weekend, that was one thing which Joel had made time for, so he should be prepared when the time came for him to be her birth partner.

Darcy began to panic slightly. It was already dusk and starting to drizzle. She could see a lot of blurry headlights through the rain-smattered windscreen, but felt totally disconnected from the outside world. She tried phoning Joel – straight to voicemail. *Perhaps he's on his way home?* Darcy wondered.

The pain retreated quickly, and Darcy built up the courage to drive on. She had just started indicating to pull back into the stream of traffic, when she felt a trickle down her leg.

Oh no! I didn't make it to the bathroom in time! Darcy began to sob, an all-too-regular occurrence fuelled by her pregnancy hormones! *I can't believe I've wet myself. My poor car seat...*

It dawned on her suddenly that the trickle had become a gush, and she was now sitting in quite a pool.

Oh my goodness! Oh my goodness! My waters! Darcy panicked, grabbing her phone again and trying Joel once more. Still no reply, she left a sobbing message, probably unintelligible through her tears.

There was only one thing for it, Darcy decided, and called the number on her medical notes. She had been told by her midwife to always keep them with her at this late stage, just in case. She spoke to a lovely lady at the birthing unit, who said she'd arrange an ambulance right away. Darcy didn't hear the rest, as she was struck again by the searing pain of another contraction. She timed this one, fifty-five seconds.

Please, not yet, she prayed quietly to herself, as the hurting subsided.

Anger began to replace Darcy's tears. *Where was Joel? Who on earth lets their phone go to voicemail when their wife is about to give birth at any moment? Where had he been nearly every evening last week?*

Darcy loved Joel and trusted him implicitly. But this was just too much. *What was she meant to think?* Okay, as their pregnancy had progressed, so their intimacy had decreased, but surely that was normal? This was their first child, so the reality of the changes in Darcy's body and in their relationship had been a bit of a shock for both of them. But that didn't give him the right to just check out whenever he pleased!

As she began breathing through another pain, Darcy saw the flashing light stop behind her. Relief flooded her, as the paramedic knocked on her window.

Rushed by ambulance to the birthing unit, Darcy was welcomed by a midwife who she had met on her tour of the facility a few weeks before. She burst into renewed crying as they led her inside.

'Do you have someone with you?' the nurse asked.

'I can't get hold of him!' Darcy shouted, not directly at the nurse, just at the situation in general.

In her labour room, and having been checked and found to be six centimetres dilated, Darcy finally began to relax. *There's still time, there's still time for him to get here.*

Her kind paramedics had brought her hospital bag in the ambulance with them. Thank goodness for being prepared! They had wished her a Merry Christmas, as they left the hospital for their next patient, which had made Darcy more tearful, wishing her mum was here. She had phoned her parents, and they were on their way, but it was a four-hour drive ordinarily from their home in Wales, longer at this time of year.

Finally paying attention to her surroundings, Darcy saw that there was a small string of Father Christmas bunting stuck on the bare hospital wall, and her drinking water had been poured into a festive cardboard cup with a reindeer on the side. She appreciated these small, homely touches.

Just then her phone buzzed. Darcy answered the call to Joel, who sounded beside himself with worry.

'Oh my goodness, Dar, I got your message. I was out of signal...'

'Out of signal, at work?' Darcy questioned, incredulously.

Seemingly ignoring her, or pretending he hadn't heard, Joel rushed on, 'Baby, what's happened?'

'What do you think has happened, Joel?' she shrieked into the handset, 'I went into labour! It doesn't take a rocket scientist...'

'Oh no, no, no, are you at home still?'

'I wasn't even at home when my waters broke!' Darcy could feel her anger rising as another contraction took hold. The midwife who was checking her vital signs took the phone from Darcy.

'Your wife is in the hospital, Mr. Franklin,' she said calmly, 'Please come to the birthing unit as soon as possible.'

Darcy was sure she heard Joel swear as the call ended, but that was so out of character, she decided she must have imagined it in her pain.

'Your husband said he'll be here in under an hour,' the kind nurse reassured her.

'Under an hour?' Darcy asked, 'But he works fifteen minutes away!'

'Maybe I misheard,' the woman added quickly, leaving Darcy as she went to attend to her next patient.

Fifty minutes later, a very frazzled Joel arrived, soaked from the rain and clearly stressed. Darcy heard him before she saw him, as he was at the nurses' station asking for her room number.

Entering her room, he rushed to the bedside, enveloping her in a hug, and kissing her cheek.

'Darcy, love, I'm so sorry, I'm so sorry.'

Darcy didn't have time to delve deeper into his apology as the contractions were coming thick and fast now. She had just been examined and was up to nine centimetres. When she'd told Joel this, he was shocked.

'I thought first babies take hours, like a whole day or something?' he asked.

'I guess ours is impatient.' Darcy answered, coolly. She wasn't sure what to think and certainly didn't have the head space for it right now. She needed Joel there, wanted him there with her, so decided to leave her questions until later.

Two hours later, two memorable hours which neither Darcy nor Joel would ever forget, and their baby boy was safely delivered. They had chosen not to find out their baby's gender until this moment, and Joel wept when he saw his son for the first time, showering Darcy in kisses. He had been a fantastic birth partner, remembering everything they had been taught.

'One last push!' Joel had shouted when the midwife told him to give Darcy a final word of encouragement. And sure enough, little Jamie Franklin had entered the world at that moment, before screaming heartily to announce his arrival.

Darcy was understandably exhausted, and lay back in her bed, watching Joel dote on their son. *He'll make a great dad,* she thought to herself. Jamie had a little knitted Christmas pudding hat sitting cosily around his tiny head, which the midwife had said was provided by the ladies of the local Women's Institute.

By now it was the middle of the night, so Darcy was settled down for some much-needed sleep after giving baby Jamie a lovely feed. Joel was asked to leave as it was the policy in the unit that only the mothers and babies could stay overnight.

Darcy felt bereft at the thought of him leaving. As tired as she was, her insecurities returned in full force, and she began crying uncontrollably again. Joel was at her side in an instant, stroking her wet hair away from her forehead and whispering how proud he was of her and how he had never loved her more than in that moment.

As it had been a quiet shift for the midwives, they took pity on the couple and let Joel stay, as long as he slept in the armchair. Darcy was running on pure adrenaline and, try as she might, she could not rest. They both sat for a long time, staring at their precious gift. Taking turns holding his little form as he slept peacefully.

'Joel?' Darcy began hesitantly, 'I know this probably isn't the time, but I need to know.'

She saw him tense. But he didn't refuse her the conversation they needed to have.

'I know what you want to discuss,' he began, 'and before I tell you, I want you to know that it was never meant to go on this long or to upset you in any way.'

'You're worrying me, Jo,' Darcy admitted in a whisper.

'No, no, please, it's nothing to be worried about. I just feel like such a fool.' He rushed on, desperate now to give his explanation.

'Three months ago I had the grand idea to get you an eternity ring,' Joel said ruefully, 'You know, for the birth of our first baby. Then a colleague said her uncle Geoff had a workshop and gave classes where people could learn how to make their own jewellery. He's a proper silversmith, and so I looked him up. It seemed perfect, so much more meaningful, designing it and then making it myself,' Joel was holding Darcy's hands, looking her in the eyes earnestly.

'Only thing was,' he continued, 'it turns out I have no talent in metal working whatsoever. Zilch. Nada. Everything took much, much longer than expected and, well, I ended up with a tight deadline. Geoff offered to finish the ring for me, but typically stubborn me, I refused, and insisted I see it through to the bitter end. It should have been complete weeks ago, but in the end, I had to go and collect it today, once the polishing was finished.'

Darcy stared at him open-mouthed – torn between adoration and annoyance.

'So, you're basically telling me, that you neglected our relationship and me, to produce a piece of jewellery?' she asked harshly.

Joel looked suitably crestfallen. 'I know, I was stupid,' he admitted, 'I just refused to quit.'

Looking at their gorgeous new baby, Darcy decided that some things were decidedly more important than others. She breathed out, slowly, making him suffer a bit longer!

'Well, let's see it then!' she encouraged, to Joel's clear relief.

The ring was certainly beautiful, an intricate Celtic design around the band, and a large piece of greeny-blue sea glass nestling in the centre.

'Is that the...'

'Yes!' Joel answered happily, 'It's the sea-glass we found the afternoon I proposed on the beach!'

'Wow!' Darcy exclaimed, turning the precious object over between her fingers.

'It's a good job your fingers swelled so much and you had to take your wedding band off,' Joel laughed, pleased with her reaction to his work, 'I had to sneak it away to find out your ring size!'

Darcy placed her palm against his cheek and kissed him slowly on the lips, thankful for the familiar pressure.

'I've missed you,' she whispered, before kissing him again, 'Now let me sleep!'

As dawn shone through the blinds, Joel said a prayer of thanks for his beautiful little family, the most precious Christmas gift of all.

9. TWO LEFT FEET

Debbie shut the door of the dance studio behind the last little ballerina and heaved a sigh of relief.

'Bye, Miss Deborah,' she could hear the giggling voices echoing down the hallway, as they headed for the exit.

Phew! Debbie was not normally eager to say goodbye to her students, but this was the last morning of classes before Christmas. Excitement levels had been through the roof, especially since she had let her youngest two classes dress up their leotards in advance of the class, with festive additions.

In hindsight, that had been her first mistake. Random baubles, glittery and feathery hairbands, and cotton wool home-made snowmen kept flying off as they danced, littering the floor and causing a trip hazard. Debbie's second mistake had been to promise them gingerbread cookies and fizzy drinks at the rest break. For the remainder of the class, attention had dwindled whilst toilet trips had skyrocketed.

Lesson learned, Debbie decided, yawning. She had been up even earlier than usual. She normally woke at six, and practised yoga before her shower. This morning, however, Debbie had been on the phone to her ex-boyfriend at four thirty in the morning. He had recently moved to America and was now eight hours behind her. Tony had called her before he went to bed, drunk as usual, and pleading once more for forgiveness.

Debbie had already decided that the best gift she could give herself this year was freedom from that toxic relationship. Tony had argued, in that incoherent, disjointed way that drunks have, but his protestations fell on deaf ears. A long-distance relationship would have been one thing, and perhaps they could have made that work, but his repeated infidelity and reliance on the whisky bottle had pushed her too far. Debbie eventually hung up, after telling him in no uncertain terms, for the third time that week, that it was over.

Two years of her life down the pan. At thirty-three, she couldn't afford to waste any more time. Having come from a broken home, with a drunken father and a narcissistic mother, Debbie was determined to bring her future children into a stable, safe home.

Finding the right partner, though, now that was the tricky thing. You didn't often seem to meet nice men randomly when out and about. Online dating was a big no-no. Debbie had too many friends who had gone down that route and had their fingers (and for some, their bank balances) burned in the process. No, she preferred more traditional methods.

Checking the large clock on the studio wall, Debbie saw that she had twenty minutes before she had to leave for her next appointment. After quickly clearing the floor of any remaining paraphernalia, she let her body begin moving, starting slowly, then faster, choosing her own rhythm and style. This was Debbie's therapy and her raison d'être. No music was necessary, she flowed to the beat of her heart.

Graceful yet intense, despite her age Debbie was still at the peak of fitness and flexibility. Her lithe, muscular frame was often commented on by her friends, in joking envy, which Debbie brushed off modestly, 'I dance for a living, what do you expect!'

Half an hour later, Debbie pulled up in the car park of Grace Retirement Village. It was a fairly new complex, with blocks of apartments encircling a centre building that had a dining hall, sitting rooms, and music room. Debbie smiled to herself. Sometimes her job took her in a strange direction and this was certainly one of those times. She had been contacted the previous month by a lovely older lady, asking if she would help her and her fiancé learn a dance routine for their wedding in the spring. Debbie had been quick to accept, and this was to be their third lesson.

She had felt embarrassed the previous week when the love ballad they had chosen made her cry a little. Too much bottled-up from her own breakup, Debbie had explained to them. However, if anyone could renew her hope in love it was Doris and Bob, such a cute couple!

Doris was waiting for her in reception as always, though Bob was as yet nowhere to be seen.

'Hello dear,' Doris gave her a sweet kiss on the cheek, 'a couple of things to report, I'm afraid!'

'Oh, I hope it's nothing serious?' Debbie asked kindly.

'No, no, it's just that Bob is a bit under the weather – a cold that's all, but he doesn't feel like dancing today.'

'I'm sorry to hear that,' Debbie replied, genuinely sad as she loved working with the pair.

'Ah, but nothing to be sad about!' Doris continued merrily, 'You see, I had forgotten that today was the Christmas tea party for us residents. You're just in time! And don't worry about not having a date, I've invited my grandson, Matthew, to join us!' Doris was buzzing with excitement, clearly very happy with herself.

Debbie was not so happy. She didn't want to appear rude, but the thought of a blind date at a retirement home dance was not high on her 'must do before Christmas' list. She smiled weakly, about to make her excuses and leave, when a very dashing man stopped alongside them. Dressed in chinos, with a smart shirt and Christmas tie, he certainly looked the part.

'And here he is now, the man himself!' Mavis said, accepting the proffered kiss and taking hold of his arm.

'Debbie, meet my grandson Matthew! Isn't he a looker!'

'Grandma!' Matthew interrupted her before she could continue singing his praises. He was blushing and clearly feeling awkward.

'Now, now, I'm allowed!' Mavis continued happily, 'Once you're over eighty, no-one expects you to have a filter!' she chuckled to herself.

Matthew raised his eyebrows in a look of rueful apology and held out his hand to Debbie,

'Matthew Carpenter,' he said, shaking her hand gently, 'Pleased to meet you.'

'And I you,' Debbie responded, letting her guard down slightly. At least he wasn't sleazy like Tony.

Debbie was suddenly very aware that she was standing there in green Lycra dance leggings and a tight red t-shirt – not exactly tea dance attire! She had, thankfully, removed the hairband which she'd worn for her morning classes, which sported two reindeer heads bobbing up and down – very classy! *Never mind, he'll have to take me as he finds me, or not at all!*

Before either had a chance to converse further, Doris ushered them both into the dining room. The tables had been moved to the edges of the room to allow for dancing, whilst a small band had set up in the corner. They were currently playing 'White Christmas,' whilst a singer who must have been at least seventy, and was clearly going for the Elvis Presley look, quiff and all, was crooning away. A few couples swayed away on the dance floor, mostly residents paired with the care workers, and an elderly man in a wheelchair danced at the edge of the scene with a lady whom Debbie recognised as his wife.

Ballroom dancing wasn't actually Debbie's cup of tea, but she decided that, since she was here, she might as well enjoy it.

'Off you go, dears!' Doris encouraged, taking Debbie's hand and putting it on Matthew's arm. With no choice but to agree, as neither wanted to upset Doris, they walked out onto the makeshift dance floor.

Once there, Matthew stood immobile, until Debbie put her left hand on his, her other hand on his shoulder, and tried to move the pair.

'I'm so sorry,' he mumbled, 'I truly do have two left feet. I apologise in advance if I squash your toes. My grandmother told me I was coming here to take some Christmas photos for her and Bob!'

'Please don't worry, Mathew,' Debbie tried to reassure him, 'this isn't my best dancing style either!'

'At least you have co-ordination!' Matthew said, tripping over his own foot, 'And please call me Matt – Matthew is my Sunday name reserved for my grandparents!'

Debbie smiled, starting to relax. His honesty was refreshing, and he certainly looked cute as he screwed up his face trying to concentrate on moving around the floor without any bumps. When a faster rendition of 'Here comes Santa Claus' began, they both retreated to the refreshment table.

'What can I get you?' Matt asked, eyeing up the offering of soft drinks and tea caddy, 'there doesn't seem to be anything alcoholic.'

'I'll take a tea, please, 'Debbie said, perhaps cooler than was necessary, 'I'm teetotal anyway.'

'Me too,' Matt agreed, flashing her a grin, 'never got a taste for the stuff, and it wasn't allowed in our home growing up – Salvation Army, you see.'

He handed her a cup of tea, in a pretty china cup, and poured himself a coke. Debbie smiled, feeling bad for being snippy.

Surprised, Debbie spotted Bob sitting at a far table with Doris, They poured some hot drinks for the old couple and carried them over.

'I thought you were a bit unwell, Bob?' Debbie enquired, one eyebrow raised.

'He, ah, he made a miraculous recovery!' Mavis cut in, at least having the decency to look a bit sheepish! Poor Bob had clearly not been party to her scheming and looked decidedly bemused.

'Well, I'm so happy to see you,' Debbie said, genuinely smiling at the older lovebirds.

She and Matt spent most of the afternoon on the dance floor, and Debbie had to admit she'd enjoyed it. Once he relaxed, Matt did manage to dance quite smoothly, and any misplaced steps were met with giggles from the two of them.

'Ah look at that!' Doris said in a stage whisper to Bob, so all could hear, 'My job here is done!'

Matt shook his head and looked down into Debbie's eyes. She noticed for the first time that although his eyes were grey, they were outlined in deep blue. Mesmerizing, in fact. She couldn't seem to look away.

Matt bent his head lower, and for a moment Debbie thought he might kiss her, but instead his put his mouth next to her ear and whispered, 'Would you like to get something to eat with me?'

Debbie nodded, not actually wanting him to pull away quite yet. When he stood up again, the side of her face felt too cold.

They said their goodbyes to Doris and Bob, who had both retreated to their armchairs in the beautiful sitting room. Decorated in reds and golds, with a tall, real fir tree in the bay window, it was a cosy bolthole away from the festivities next door.

Doris kissed them both on the cheek and whispered in Debbie's ear, 'He's a good one!'

'I know, I worked that much out!' Debbie whispered back, 'Thank you!'

As they walked out, Debbie asked Matt if she could meet him at the restaurant, as she wanted to have a shower and get changed into something more suitable. They agreed to meet at seven o'clock at a small Italian restaurant near her cottage.

When Debbie arrived, Matt was already waiting outside. He had brought her a small posy of red roses decorated with tiny white seed pearls on stalks. Debbie was touched. It had been a long time since she'd received a gift from a man. She was equally touched by Matt's expression – his eyes were on stalks when he saw her, even though she was wearing a simple black midi dress with red heels.

The restaurant was crowded with Christmas office parties and friends catching up before the holidays. Luckily, Matt had called ahead, and a small table in the window had been reserved for them. The window was lit up with fairy lights, which complemented the candlelight on each table.

Matt pulled Debbie's chair out for her, kissing her lightly on the cheek as she sat down.

I hope he's not too good to be true! Debbie worried silently.

Despite her natural inclination to be cautious, Debbie entered the evening with an open mind, which compensated for her very fragile heart. Conversation flowed easily between them, as did chemistry.

Without a shadow of a doubt, the pair were attracted to each other. Amongst shy looks of attraction when they thought the other wasn't looking, their laughter bubbled up unguarded and Debbie could not remember having had a better date.

Skipping dessert, they opted instead for a cinnamon latte from the local coffee shop. Walking along arm in arm, drinks keeping their fingers warm, Matt suddenly stopped and turned to face Debbie.

Nervously, he took the drink out of her hand and put both cups down on the garden wall of the house behind them. He reached out to take both of Debbie's hands in his, and spoke softly, so that she had to strain to hear him.

'I know we've only just met,' he began,' but I feel like I've known you for a very long time. I want you to know how much I've enjoyed your company this evening.'

Debbie nodded in agreement, 'Me too,' she whispered. Waiting hopefully for the kiss that she wished would come next, Debbie looked at Matt expectantly. He searched her eyes in return, apparently looking for some sign or signal that his attentions were welcomed.

Debbie was not the most patient of people and could only take so much of this build up. It was like sweet, sweet torture. Taking matters into her own hands, she reached up on tiptoes. Being only five feet two tall, Matt was about a foot taller than her. Thankfully, he began to bend down, smiling until they were standing with the tips of their noses touching.

Finding his courage, Matt closed the remainder of the distance between them, his lips landing on hers with a feather-like delicacy. It was the merest brush, just a hint of what could be between them. Debbie moved hers slightly in response, resting there until they both craved more friction between them.

The butterflies in Debbie's stomach turned to fireworks as their passion grew. She had reached her arms around Matt's waist, and when their mouths pulled away, their bodies remained close together. They swayed gently, in an ode to their dancing earlier in the day.

Was that only today? Debbie wondered, feeling like she had known him forever.

Neither being in a rush to leave the other, they took their time walking to their cars. The air around them was cold, but the heat between them hadn't diminished.

'I'd really like to see you again,' Matt said, hesitantly.

'How about tomorrow?' Debbie asked. He grinned and kissed her again.

He may have two left feet, Debbie thought, *but I'm really going to enjoy taking one step at a time with him!* She kissed him responsively in return, leaving Matt in no doubt that there would be many more dates to come.

10. HOME IS WHERE THE SNOWMAN IS

Lauren opened her eyes slowly, sinking further into the mattress and under her duvet to avoid the chill in her bedroom. She had absolutely no motivation to get up and face the day. On the agenda for today, it being Christmas Eve, was a mountain of cooking, preparation and organisation. She didn't know if she could face it.

The sound of little feet pitter-patting across the wooden floor signalled that any time for procrastination was over. A little blonde head appeared over the edge of her bed, followed by a wriggly little body and two stubby legs.

'Morning, Tiger!' Lauren said with all the enthusiasm she could muster, trying to stifle a yawn.

'Shanta?' the little boy asked, hopefully, his eyes shining in barely suppressed excitement as he bounced up and down on the double bed.

'No Billy, S-anta isn't coming today. One more sleep!'

Crestfallen, Billy snuggled down beside his mum and watched as she checked her text messages.

Lauren was on edge. She should have heard from Gav by now. Tomorrow was Christmas Day for goodness sake! She had fourteen family members coming round for turkey with all the trimmings, trifle and the Queen's speech. He was meant to be home two days ago.

Smiling at Billy to disguise her worry, Lauren said, 'Let's get some breakfast, shall we?'

'Choclik?' Billy asked, giggling.

'No, you know it's banana, porridge or toast! Nice try though, little guy!' She ruffled his fluffy hair and was struck by how much he was starting to look like Gavin. Same blue eyes, same cheeky grin. Her husband wouldn't recognise their son when he got home. After seven months away in Saudi Arabia fixing oil pipelines, she could barely remember what it was like to have him home.

Checking my phone every five minutes, won't help! Lauren chided herself, getting out of bed and reaching for her dressing gown. The blizzard that had been raging all day yesterday had finally stopped, leaving a thick layer of snow over the garden and street outside.

Billy raced to the French doors in the kitchen, pointing outside, 'Shnow!' he exclaimed.

'Yes, Sweetpea, we'll go out in the s-now later, when Mummy has finished a few jobs. Do you want to watch Paw Patrol while you eat your banana?'

With Billy snuggled on the sofa, Lauren rushed to get dressed and start ticking things off her 'To Do' list. She decided to do the worst things first, so that the day would hopefully get easier as it progressed.

'Ok, number one,' she said aloud to Billy, who was now playing with his train track, the remains of his breakfast mushed into the carpet, and his TV programme long forgotten, 'Table settings.'

Lauren was struggling with this supposedly simple task, it was worse than the top table at a wedding! Her mum couldn't be left next to her Aunt Greta, because a couple of sherries between them and they'd be bickering like teenagers again. Little Josh was a no-go sitting with his big sister, Heidi, as he would pull her hair constantly making her yelp and their mum (Lauren's sister) would spend the whole meal shouting at them. Finally, her mother-in law couldn't sit beside Lauren's dad, as she thought it was acceptable to flirt outrageously with him, even though Lauren's mum was right there.

Arrgghh! Lauren decided to put the names in a jar and pull them out one by one. That would be the order around the table and she was not going to alter it. *Big tick, move on!*

Making the trifle. *How hard could this be?* Lauren wondered. She had seen her mum make it many times over the years, it couldn't be that difficult. Apparently, Billy wanted to help with this one too – anything involving food and he was there in an instant, climbing onto his little step stool to reach the top of the counter. It would have probably been both quicker and more successful, if she had not had a little sous-chef, and if she had bothered to search for a recipe online. Never mind, Lauren ploughed on and managed to get the jellied sponge and fruit into the fridge to set, leaving herself a note to add the custard, fresh cream and toppings later.

Billy was by now desperate to get outside. Wrapped in his winter woollens, with coat, hat, scarf and mittens, he stood by the door, saying 'Shnowman, shnowman,' on repeat until Lauren managed to pull on her boots and coat.

'Yes, let's build a s-nowman,' Lauren said, her teeth already chattering in the icy air.

Twenty minutes later, hearing her phone ringing but unable to leave Billy unattended, Lauren scooped him up and rushed indoors. Indignant at having to leave his masterpiece with no stick arms or carrot nose, Billy began squealing. Trying to placate him, Lauren did not get to the call in time.

'Oh no!' she exclaimed, seeing that the missed call was from an unknown number and the caller had left no message. She tried to phone them back immediately, but it went straight to a generic voicemail.

Fighting back the tears, Lauren distracted herself with fussing over Billy, promising him they could go back out later and finish the snowman once they'd both warmed up a bit. They might even use one of Daddy's scarves to dress him up a bit – this cheered Billy up no end and he started pottering about with his trains again.

The day plodded on with almost unbearable slowness. Billy helped Lauren to set the table, and to find enough chairs from around the house. They listened to Christmas tunes and finished their snowman in the garden. Lauren was exhausted. Her constant tension was giving her a headache and leaving her with aching muscles and little patience.

'You're such a good little helper!' she praised her son, not wanting to spoil this day for him, 'Let's get some chocolate milk!'

Lauren made herself a fancy coffee from the machine Gav had bought her last Christmas. She loved coffee, especially made from freshly pressed beans and frothy milk. She had just sat down with Billy to enjoy her drink when a phone call from her mum nearly tipped Lauren over the edge.

'Your father and I were thinking we could come and stay the night, to help you with the final preparations, putting the Santa presents out, and to see Billy when he wakes on Christmas morning,' she stated, less in request than as if it were a done deal.

The idea in itself was a kind one, but Lauren couldn't get away from the feeling that it should be her and Gavin doing those things, not her with her parents. She wasn't a teenager any more, she was a married woman of twenty-nine! Lauren felt resentful and cross, and struggled to hide it from her voice.

'Mum, I don't need extra help, I'm managing just fine!'

'I'm sure you are dear, it certainly sounds like it!' this raised Lauren's heckles even further, 'We just want to be with our grandson on Christmas Eve, to see him putting his little carrot out for the reindeer and his tipple for Father Christmas.'

Lauren knew she had no choice of refusing without causing an argument, so she agreed that they could come over after supper and stay the night in the guest bedroom.

Billy was beyond excited by this point. At almost three years old, this was the first Christmas that he had really understood what was happening and so could anticipate the gifts and joy to come. They had visited Santa's Grotto in the local garden centre the previous weekend, and the big man himself had promised Billy a new train track. He had been in awe at meeting Santa Claus himself, and had not stopped chatting about it since.

Billy splashed his way through bath time, singing 'Jingle Bells' at the top of his voice, ran around with his new reindeer pyjamas wrapped around his head as Lauren tried to dry him, and screamed through the window at the neighbour's cat, who had come to investigate their snowman. Billy had named the snowman Daddy, because he was wearing Daddy's scarf. Lauren had not had the heart to suggest an alternative name.

At six o'clock, Lauren's parents arrived, arms laden with food and gifts. Their presents for Billy had been left in the car boot until he was safely asleep.

'Here dear, put this trifle in the fridge!' Mum commanded from the hallway.

'Actually, I said I was going to make the trifle,' Lauren replied indignantly, already exasperated. Their arrival had caused Billy to become excited again when it was almost his bedtime.

'I know you did! I just thought I'd bring a back-up!' Lauren tried to smile gratefully through gritted teeth, took the dessert and retreated to the kitchen. She could hold it back no longer, and began crying, silent tears running down her cheeks.

'Now what's this?' her mum asked, joining her, 'it's silly to get upset over a pudding!'

'Of course I'm not upset over a trifle!' Lauren shouted, louder than was probably necessary.

She asked her dad to watch the Christmas episode of Thomas the Tank Engine with Billy and retreated upstairs to compose herself.

I might as well make the most of the adult help, Lauren decided, and went to take a shower in an attempt to drown out her anxiety.

Coming out of the bathroom, her towel wrapped around her curvy frame, and her hair wet and pinned up on top of her head, Lauren froze in the doorway to the bedroom. At first, she thought she must be imagining it, the man sitting on the bed, taking off his boots. But no, it really was him.

'Gavin!' she exclaimed, 'When did you get here? Where have you been?'

'Oh, Hi,' he replied, flashing her his signature grin and standing up to welcome Lauren into his arms, looking her up and down appreciatively.

'Your mother let me in, five minutes ago, she had a few choice words to say about how worried you were – 'on an emotional edge,' apparently. I sneaked up before Billy saw me – I have some gifts for him I didn't want him to see. Then I heard you in the shower and my homecoming got a lot sweeter!' He winked at her in the flirty way she both loved and hated. Normally, he used it to get out of any disagreement, and to persuade her into bed! She hadn't seen it for so long, it would have made her weak at the knees were she not still piqued over the worry Gav had caused her.

'Why no phone call for two weeks? Why cutting it so fine for

Christmas?' She asked, resting her head on his chest. He was still in his coat, and it was wet from another snowfall. It didn't matter, she was wet from the shower anyway, and she needed to feel that he was really there.

'The usual, delays finishing the contract, problems with transport at the Saudi end, flight cancellations, snowstorms in Europe, losing my phone charger... I did try to call you earlier from a colleague's mobile, to say I'd reached Heathrow, but there was no answer.'

Lauren decided she didn't want a post mortem of his delay. Not in that moment anyway. She wanted him.

She looked up at her husband and smiled, 'I'm so happy to have you home,' she said, relief making her emotional, 'Kiss me!'

Gavin didn't need to be asked twice. He caught her lips with all the hunger from their long separation and ran his hands through her wet hair. She stripped him out of his coat and shirt and let him unhook her towel. It slipped to the ground in a puddle, forgotten in their urgent explorations. They poured all of their emotions, all of their longing and loneliness into their lovemaking. What it lacked in finesse and duration, they made up for in intensity.

Lying in Gav's arms a short time later, Lauren told him all of Billy's news, finishing with their day.

'Well, I'll have to see this Daddy Snowman!' Gavin said contentedly, and spend some time with my little Mini-Me before bedtime.'

'It's already long past his bedtime,' Lauren replied, 'so I don't think another half an hour will matter!'

They dressed and went downstairs to surprise Billy.

'Dadada!' his shouted, running squealing into Gavin's arms. Gavin picked him up and swung him around, showering kisses over his chubby cheeks.

'Little Bud! I hear someone special is paying us a visit tonight?'

'It's Shanta!' Billy said authoritatively, pointing to the picture in the book his Grandpa was reading, 'The Night Before Christmas'.

'Yes, and I hear you made a special person in the garden for me?'

'Daddy shnowman!' Billy rushed to the French doors in the

kitchen. It was dark outside, but the light from indoors illuminated the white figure, still smart in his woolly scarf.

'You did a great job, Billy!' Gavin praised the little boy, whose eyes glowed in adoration of his hero, 'I'm so proud of you for looking after mummy while I was away!'

Lauren and Gavin took time with Billy's bedtime, both tucking him into his little infant bed and pulling his blankets up around him.

'Straight to sleep now,' Lauren urged him, caressing Billy's cheek, 'so that Santa Claus can come with his reindeer!'

Sneaking back downstairs so as not to disturb the little boy, the pair found her mum and dad putting their gifts under the beautifully decorated tree.

'Sorry about earlier, Mum' Lauren apologised, 'That reminds me, Gav! I've a job for you!' she kissed him lovingly on the cheek.

'Oh?' Gavin replied, curious at the teasing tone in her voice.

'Yes, Mum and I need a blindfolded taste-tester for some trifles!'

'I wouldn't wish that job on anyone!' Lauren's dad added, laughing, 'It's a no-win situation!'

They walked into the kitchen together, Lauren leading Gav by the hand as, for some reason, this was one request he seemed rather reluctant to fulfil!

11. SILENT NIGHT

Olivia stepped back to admire her handiwork. She had to admit, the pulpit was looking particularly festive this year. Fresh holly cut from her garden, sprigs of ivy from the bush at the side of her house, red roses and silver ribbon had all combined to produce a beautiful Christmas display. Olivia was proud of her work. The other members of the church flower-arranging group had tended to look down on Olivia's creations, seeing her as inexperienced. *They must base this on my age,* Olivia thought, as at forty-seven she was the youngest in the group by a decade. Reverend Jim always seemed pleased with her efforts, though, as did the parishioners.

Only a few poinsettias and remote-controlled plastic candles to dot around the deep, high window ledges in the main body of the building, and she would be finished. Olivia went through to the church hall to look for a ladder in the large storage cupboard, which housed everything from Sunday School crafts to tins of paint and packets of custard cream biscuits.

Her back to the hall, Olivia jumped when a voice behind her said,

'Hello, Olivia ... Sorry, I didn't mean to startle you!'

Turning to face the voice, Olivia knew instantly that it would be Philip. She recognised the sound of the man who was at once as familiar to her as a well-worn glove, and at the same time almost a stranger.

She had been surprised one Sunday morning a few months earlier, when Philip had been introduced to the congregation as the new caretaker for their small parish church. To be fair, the building was over a hundred years old and needed quite a lot of upkeep, having lasted without a janitor for two years since the previous holder of the role had retired. Nevertheless, the sight of him in that church service, after all these years, had shocked Olivia more than she had liked to admit – especially to herself.

'Hello, Philip,' she replied, smiling politely and walking towards him, ladders in hand.

'Here, let me carry that for you!' he exclaimed, rushing forward to take the load from her.

They walked back into the main church together, neither knowing quite what to say. This was the first time they had been alone in twenty-five years. Of course, they had exchanged pleasantries during coffee after the services these past months, but only a few sentences each time at most.

Directing him where to stand the ladders, Olivia thanked Philip for his help, trying not to sound awkward and stilted.

'Can I make you a coffee?' Philip asked kindly, 'I'm having a break before I decorate the tree that's just been delivered. Why the vicar ordered a seven-foot monster, I'm not sure! That'll be a lot of pine needles to sweep up when they all drop!'

Olivia remembered his dry sense of humour well and knew that he was only joking. As far as she recalled, he loved the season of Advent.

'Yes, please, that would be lovely,' she replied, before adding, 'I have time to help you with the tree, if you like?' No-one was more surprised than Olivia at her offer. *What am I thinking?* she wondered, but the words were already spoken.

'That would be great, amazing in fact!' Philip seemed genuinely grateful for her offer, and smiled, the action making the laughter lines around his eyes crinkle expressively. He looked a lot different to the last time she had seen him, of course, greyer and broader, but still with that innate bearing of confidence and calm. Olivia clearly remembered waving Philip off at the train station in Durham, the last time she had seen him in her youth. Their studies complete, final exams passed successfully, degree certificates achieved and celebrated, and he off to work in Nottingham.

They had met in Freshers' Week at Durham university, and were pretty much inseparable from that day onwards. For three years, amongst his History studies, and her English Literature classes, they had partied together, shared their lives together and loved one another with a force that was as scary as it was exhilarating. A true rollercoaster of emotions.

'Here you go!' Philip said, returning a few minutes later with their hot drinks, 'I hope you still like milk in it?'

'Yes, that's perfect thank you,' Olivia responded, climbing down from her perch and accepting the chipped mug from him.

'Shall we have a seat in one of the pews while we take a break?' Philip asked, for once sounding unsure.

'Yes, I suppose so, thanks,' Olivia replied, somewhat reluctantly.

Sitting on the same bench, separated by their cups, Olivia and Philip stared ahead in uncomfortable silence. Philip cleared his throat, 'Libbie, I'm sorry.'

It was said so quietly, that Olivia could have been forgiven for thinking she had misheard. However, the use of his pet name for her convinced her that she had definitely heard correctly.

'Don't Philip, please don't,' she said, harshly, struggling to keep the bitterness from her voice, 'it was a very long time ago.'

'I know that, Lib, I know, but I've waited a long time to say this. I'm so sorry I hurt you. I hurt myself just as much.'

'How would you know how much you hurt me? You didn't speak to me after the phone call where you told me you wanted some 'space' to 'live your life a bit,' WITHOUT ME,' Olivia was almost shouting now. He had effectively ripped the stitches open on an old wound and exposed it to the air again.

'I was a fool, a young, stupid, fool,' Philip continued remorsefully, 'I thought the grass would be greener, that I should play the field a bit, my Dad told me I was mad to settle down with the first girl I was serious about. And neither of us wanted a long-distance relationship,' he added for good measure.

'You moved to Nottingham, Phil, not New Zealand!'

Taking a deep breath, Olivia continued more calmly, 'It really doesn't matter any more.'

'Did you marry, Libbie?' The question made her anger boil over again.

'How is that any of your business? I don't think that it is. But no, for your information, no. I didn't live like a nun, by any means, but I didn't marry any of them.' She turned away, to hide the fury and hurt in her eyes.

'Me neither, me neither,' he said softly, sadly, 'No-one compared to you. You set the bar too high. You were always the one for me.' Philip reached over to take Olivia's hand, but she anticipated the action and snatched it away before their skin touched.

It was too much, all too much.

Standing up abruptly and nearly knocking over their coffees in the process, Olivia walked back over to the ladders to finish her task. Working silently, she heard Philip behind her taking their still-full cups to the kitchenette in the corner.

Not wanting to invite more conversation, Olivia tidied up quickly, grabbed her coat and handbag, and left. The cold air outside was a welcome relief for her overheated senses. She took several deep breaths and hoped her usual composure would return. It didn't. *Why did she feel like a twenty-one-year old all over again? Why did she want to scream at him, whilst simultaneously wanting to feel his arms around her?*

It had taken her years to get to the point where she no longer shed tears over the loss of him. Years of heartache, of doubting herself, of seeking but not finding someone to fill the Philip-shaped hole in her heart.

Without conscious thought, Olivia's feet carried her back inside the church. She paused in the porch, wondering what on earth she was doing. Her inner voice was screaming incoherently.

Philip spotted her from his position at the back of the hall. He was bent over, looking into a large cardboard box which was overflowing with Christmas tree ornaments. Straightening up, he stood looking at Olivia, his shoulders drooped and his expression sombre.

Olivia approached him slowly, no idea what she was going to say.

'I've missed you Libbie,' he said when she was almost beside him, 'every year, every month, every day – more than you could ever know.'

'Do you think I haven't missed you?' she retorted, her voice sounding harsh in her own ears. 'I lost a piece of myself the day you said you no longer wanted me. I don't think I ever quite found it again, probably because it was still with you!'

Olivia dropped her bag on the ground and put her head in her hands, bending almost double. It was too much to bear. Decades of pent-up hurt and rejection exploded out of her. She began to shake, her whole body reacting to the flood of emotion. The dam wall was broken and she was wracked with wave after wave of sobs. Seeing Philip approaching cautiously, she held her hand up to tell him to come no closer. Words were impossible, such was the strength of the tidal wave assailing her.

As Olivia sank to her knees, Philip joined her on the cold parquet floor. He didn't want to ignore her wishes that he keep his distance, but at the same time his own heart ached to comfort her, the only woman he had ever loved. Tears streamed down his cheeks, seeing the suffering that he had caused them both, its truth ugly now that it was exposed and open for him to witness.

After what felt like an eternity to them both, Olivia's crying dimmed to a quiet weeping. She patted her eyes on the sleeve of her woollen coat and looked up into Philip's concerned gaze. She was moved to see that he, too, had been upset. They sat on the freezing floor staring at each other.

Is it too late to undo the hurt? Olivia wondered silently. She certainly didn't want to give either of them false hope.

'Please,' Philip whispered, 'let me hold you.'

He shuffled across until their knees touched, and leaned forwards. Olivia nodded slowly and allowed him to pull her into the circle of his embrace.

'Libbie, Libbie, Libbie,' he repeated her name over and over into her hair, as she clung to his arms as she would a raft after a shipwreck. Certainly, the storm in which they were now embroiled was not over. Far from it.

Libbie felt him kissing her head and then her face. Her common sense told her to move away, to disconnect from his touch to protect her heart. But her heart itself yearned for that very comfort which he offered. So, she stayed immobile, neither openly accepting nor rejecting his affection.

As the light touches reached her lips, however, Libbie had to make a decision. *What am I doing?* She asked herself for the umpteenth time.

Philip paused, a hairs breadth away from her mouth, silently waiting for her consent. Libbie gave the faintest of nods, easily missed had not every one of Philip's senses been focused on her.

Their kiss felt like a homecoming. Old and new, familiar and yet strange, so many emotions packed into one action, bubbling over like a kettle that had finally boiled.

Libbie gave in to the sensations and committed herself to this reconnection with her soulmate. They stayed in each other's arms, kissing, whispering long-held secrets, not wanting the moment to end. Eventually, when their legs were long numb from the cold, hard surface beneath them, and their tears dried in streaks below swollen eyes, the pair stood up.

'Where do we go from here?' Philip asked, the hope in his voice undisguisable.

'Well, I would suggest we decorate this tree,' Libbie replied, deliberately avoiding the more meaningful subtext in his question, 'Then we'll see.'

Their task complete, the pair headed out into what was now a very wintery evening. The streetlights were on, bathing the churchyard in their eerie glow.

'Would you like to go for something to eat?' Phillip enquired, taking her hand in his.

'No, no thank you, I need some time to get my thoughts straight,' Libbie smiled apologetically, 'but I'll give you my number,' she added.

Parting from him felt strangely difficult, even though Libbie had managed without his presence for over half her lifetime. Now, she felt lonely and unsettled. Getting home, she lit her wood burner and sat on the sofa under a blanket, her tabby cat, Charlie, curled up on her legs.

The next few days passed slowly. Libbie was busy at her job in the city library, where she was the Director of Literary Information. She only worked four days a week, giving her time to do the church flowers and other hobbies. Text messages flew between her and Philip, and they had even had a few Facetime calls, chatting about their present lives and past histories.

It was four thirty on Friday afternoon, when Libbie was just leaving work, that her phone rang as she walked to the metro station. She saw the call was from Philip and answered immediately.

'Hi, Libbie,' he sounded nervous, 'I was wondering if you'd like to meet me at the church later this evening – say six thirty? – the choir are practicing for their recital on Sunday.'

'Um, yes, that would be good,' Libbie replied, a bit perplexed at his request. The choir did not usually ask for an audience for their rehearsals, 'I'll see you there, then.'

She rushed home, showered and blow dried her hair, even applying a bit of make-up (which was not part of her normal routine), before heading out to church.

The old wooden door creaked as Libbie pushed it open. She was surprised to see that the main lights were off, and the whole seating area had been adorned with candles – real ones this time. Walking up the central aisle between the rows of pews, Libbie saw the choir ahead, sitting patiently, all smiling widely at her. As she reached the front near the pulpit, the choir began to sing 'Silent Night' – it was beautiful and almost other-worldly, surrounded as she was by candlelight and the flowers which she had arranged earlier that week.

Philip emerged from the side door that led to the vestry. Like her, he had made an effort and was dressed in a smart suit. Without saying a word, he came towards her, taking her hand, and then kneeling down on one knee.

Oh my goodness, he's not...

'Olivia Chapman,' he said clearly, smiling straight into her eyes, 'I have loved you since the day I met you. You are my God-given partner, the soulmate I was always meant to share my life with. I know we have a lot to work out, but we have time, and I don't want to miss another single minute of life with you. Will you do me the honour of becoming my wife?'

He held out a small, ornate box, which was open to display a perfectly formed ruby ring.

Libbie didn't let her doubts jump in, instead answering, 'Yes', without hesitation.

'Yes, my Love, I will,' she said confidently, tears streaming down her cheeks, as the choir clapped, wiping their own watery eyes.

Philip kissed her tenderly before slipping the ring onto her fourth finger. 'You've made me happier than I ever thought possible,' he whispered, 'happier than I deserve to be.'

'Shhh,' Libbie said gently, cupping his face in her palm and rubbing her thumb along his chin, 'we're together now, let's make that all that matters.'

They thanked the choir and sat in the front pew to listen to the rest of their rehearsal, hands held tightly, legs touching, faces close.

'You are, and have always been, my biggest Blessing in life,' Philip spoke softly into her ear, and Libbie squeezed his hand and said a silent prayer of thanks for her new fiancé.

12. FLIGHT OF FANCY

Marie could not think of anywhere she less wanted to be right now, than stuck in Boston Logan airport, in the middle of a snowstorm, the last Friday before Christmas. She looked at the departures board again, the list of delays and cancellations increasing. So far, her plane to London was only delayed, albeit by three hours and counting, past its scheduled take-off time.

She had already read three chapters of her chick-lit novel, drunk enough weak coffee to have her rushing to the bathroom all evening, and studiously avoided the admiring glances of a man at least twice her age, wearing a tarnished gold wedding band. Yes, she had exhausted the delights this airport had to offer.

Given that she had at least five hours to wait before boarding and didn't want to go through security yet in case her flight was completely cancelled, Marie took a walk outside. The freezing air was a welcome relief after the stuffiness of the terminal. She pulled her scarf tight and felt around in her pockets for her gloves. Without warning, a taxi pulled up at breakneck speed in front of her, splashing her feet with slush from the road, 'Hey!' Marie shouted, shaking her ankles to rid her boots of the murky droplets.

A tall, lanky figure unfolded himself from the passenger door before rushing around to grab his bag from the boot. Fumbling in his backpack, he didn't look up as he charged forwards, walking straight into Marie.

'HEY!' she shouted for the second time, standing her ground and forcing the guilty stranger to look up. He had the cheek to be looking mad at her!

'Why didn't you get out of the way?' the guy asked, clearly irritated.

'Well, I was here first!' Marie retorted, incredulous.

They stood staring at each other for a second, neither prepared to stand aside on the narrow walkway.

His eyes squinted at her in the bad lighting, 'Marie?' he asked, shock registering in his voice.

Marie had no idea how he knew her, so said nothing.

'Marie Copeland, from St. Gabriel's High?'

'Um, yes' Marie replied, even more confused as that had been a decade ago.

'It's Noah, Noah Cartwright.'

'Noah?' Marie stared more closely, trying to find a trace of the small, acne-covered teenager, in the tall, handsome man in front of her.

'You remember?' he continued, 'We had a brief thing before my dad got redeployed and we had to move to Germany!'

Ah yes, the flashbacks came screaming back to Marie now, embarrassing in their vividness. She and Noah smooching behind the dining hall, teenage fumbling at a party. Yuck!

'Yes, yes, I remember,' she said politely, moving to let him past, 'Nice to meet you again.'

'Late for my plane, I'm afraid,' Noah said apologetically, to Marie's silent relief, 'Gotta dash! Happy Christmas!'

And he was off, lurching forwards on gangly legs, a small holdall slung over his shoulder.

Marie retreated to the comfort of the coffee shop again, lest she run into any more ancient exes.

Fate was not on her side however, as a short ten minutes later, she spotted Noah there in the queue near to her. She slunk down further into her seat and tried to hide behind her tablet. No such luck.

'Hi, um, again, Marie' He stood awkwardly in front of her, tray in hand, looking hopefully at the chair opposite, 'all of the other tables are taken so I was wondering...'

His question hung in the air, and Marie simply nodded in response. He sat down, almost spilling his coffee and putting his tray down on her unopened book.

'Sorry, sorry,' Noah muttered as he rearranged the table before slipping into the chair. 'My flight is delayed by several hours, typical hey, just before Christmas an' all. Where are you headed?'

Clearly, No chance of sitting in (un)comfortable silence then? Marie asked herself. Instead, saying aloud, 'Back to Heathrow, then a hire car to Bath. You?'

'Heathrow too,' he replied, clearly happy with their shared destination. Then a quick hop up to Edinburgh to see my folks. Dad's retired now, and they have a house in the New Town area.'

'That's lovely,' Marie responded, before making a point of picking up her abandoned novel and flicking it open to a random page.

'So, what are you up to now?' Noah persevered, clearly not wanting to take the hint.

Marie put her book back on the table pointedly and sighed inwardly. This was going to be a long coffee break in more ways than one!

'Well, I work as a Personal Assistant and Events Manager for a big marketing company in Cambridge, just outside Boston,' Marie explained, 'and you?'

'I'm a youth worker in Downtown,' he began, before launching into a detailed explanation of his role. Marie was regretting her choice of caffeine over alcohol, though she smiled politely.

'… so that's why I'm single and travelling alone.' He finished, rather dejectedly.

Marie had tuned out well before the lead up to that last piece of information, so replied with a simple, 'that's a shame,' having no idea what had actually happened, and not wanting to get into the details of her own recent break-up with him.

In the space of one cup of coffee, Noah had covered his whole life story from high school to the present day, his siblings, nieces and nephews, and his parent's pet dog, Scruffy. Marie nodded and smiled, nodded and smiled. She did find him slightly cute, with his boyish eagerness to reconnect with her, and his wavy hair, wild from running his long fingers through it repeatedly. His eyes shone with genuine interest as his listened to her side of the conversation, asking questions and reacting with laughter to her anecdotes.

Despite herself, Marie began to relax. Noah had always had a great sense of humour, she remembered, and that had been the main attraction for her when they were younger. That, and the fact that he'd always had money for chocolate from the local newsagent! They stood up together to check the departures board again.

Cancelled.

Their flight had now been cancelled outright. In fact, the screen was now indicating that the blizzard had grounded all the planes until morning.

'Fantastic!' Marie said sarcastically, rather louder than she'd intended. The concourse was now heaving with people, queues forming at the airline desks to arrange alternatives.

Marie and Noah rushed side by side to the British Airways customer service area. They each had hand luggage which Noah had thoughtfully carried for them both.

Reaching the front of the line some twenty-five minutes later, the pair were disheartened to hear that the snowstorm had left roads into the city impassable and their only option was to spend the night in a local hotel. Given little choice in the matter, they both agreed, asking to be booked in on the next available flight before Christmas. They had two days to get back to the UK before the day itself, and the weather was clearly not on their side.

They packed into the hotel shuttle bus with the other disgruntled, damp travellers, all squeezed together like sardines. There were no seats left for Marie or Noah, so she found herself wedged between him and a large, bearded man, who had clearly not showered recently. Given the choice, Marie hugged close to Noah's side and he looked down at her sympathetically before raising his eyebrows in understanding. He himself was involuntarily cosied up to an older woman, who kept jabbing her handbag into his ribs to get him to move backwards, closer to Marie, so that there was now no air between their bodies.

'Happy Christmas to one and all!' Noah muttered so that only Marie could hear. She smiled in response and was grateful for his permanent good humour. Her ex, Martin, would have been huffing and puffing by now, and threatening to cancel their whole trip to visit her parents, reminding her that he had never liked England. She had always wondered, then, why he'd bothered dating an Englishwoman in the first place.

The bus pulled up outside the airport hotel, and everyone piled out. Noah and Marie watched in awe, as the tiny old lady used her handbag to ram bearded bloke in the shins and get ahead of him. They shared a glance of mutual amusement, and joined the crowd rushing to the reception desk.

The poor man attending to the angry group was clearly unprepared for this onslaught. By the time Marie and Noah reached the front of the line, he was frazzled and apologetic. His computer was working at a go-slow pace.

'Is there any chance of getting a room?' Noah asked him hopefully, 'Or is that just a flight of fancy at this point in time?'

Studying his screen closely, the man looked at Noah, to Marie, then back at Noah again.

'I have one room left,' he stated, 'so I hope you two are together!'

'Well, ah, no that's not actually the case,' Noah replied, adding, 'unfortunately' under his breath.

'Well then, we may have a small problem here,' the clerk said, looking at them both for an answer.

'It's fine,' Marie piped up, surprising herself as much as the two men, whose eyes were now all on her, 'provided it's a twin, we'll take it.'

Noah practically had to pick his jaw up off the floor, as the guy behind the counter frantically typed their details into his computer, clearly thankful that his job here was done.

Entering the small bedroom, Marie had never been so thankful for the strange American habit of placing two double beds into a room – in the UK, a twin consisted of two single beds!

Placing her small hand luggage bag on the bed closest to the window, she sat down heavily. She watched from the corner of her eye as Noah did the same.

'I'm sorry,' he said, even though none of this was his fault, 'if you like, I can leave.'

'Don't be silly!' Marie responded, 'we're both adults, we have two beds, it'll be fine.'

'I won't get undressed,' Noah reassured her.

'It's fine, really,' Marie smiled, more to convince herself than her new roommate. It suddenly dawned on her that her hand luggage contained no spare clothing, let alone pyjamas. She stood up and pulled the curtains shut. It was after eight in the evening, and pitch-black outside.

'I'm starving!' Noah exclaimed, flicking on the television to a made-for-TV Christmas movie, and kicking off his boots.

Shortly later, they decided to head down to the hotel restaurant for a bite to eat. Marie found she was glad of the company. The last six months of her relationship with Martin had left her with a large dose of anxiety, which reared its ugly head when she least expected it. This was one of those times, and Marie was grateful to Noah for filling the silence with conversation, putting her at ease again. She laughed at his silly jokes and enjoyed the festive atmosphere in the room, the tunes playing in the background and the twinkling lights.

A couple of times, she caught Noah looking at her intensely, but he either turned away or reverted to comedy whenever he was aware of her returning the gaze.

Retiring to the bar area, Marie opted for a night-cap to help her sleep, enjoying a glass of chardonnay whilst Noah had a beer. They sat by the small fire and chatted about their plans for the holidays.

'Another round?' Marie suggested, beginning to really enjoy the evening. Noah didn't need to be asked twice and quickly accepted her offer.

As the night progressed, they relaxed much more in each other's company.

'You could always come up to Edinburgh for New Year,' Noah suggested, that hopeful look back in his eyes, 'they have such great Hogmanay celebrations there!'

'I might just take you up on that offer!' Marie said, in a somewhat flirty tone, the second large glass of white having apparently gone straight to her head.

Noah blushed and grinned, giving Marie a glimpse of the teenager she had known.

Returning to their room, Marie sat down on the first bed that she came to, which happened to be Noah's. He sat right beside her and let out a long breath.

'That was a lovely evening,' he said, his voice lower and huskier than it had been earlier in the day.

'It certainly was,' Marie agreed, looking directly at him and smiling.

The air between them was electric, neither looked away, neither moved in case the spell would be broken.

Kiss me! Marie urged with her eyes, leaning imperceptibly towards him.

Noah looked at her lips, then back to her eyes, then back to her lips again.

'You know,' he said, clearing his throat, 'I'm not the kind of guy to take advantage of a beautiful, slightly tipsy woman.'

'That's a real shame,' Marie replied, before leaning in and capturing his mouth in a searing kiss. It was slow at first, Noah clearly taken aback somewhat, but he matched her wild energy soon enough and the electricity crackled around them like a log fire.

'As first kisses go, that was my best!' Marie exclaimed, the alcohol having removed her inhibitions.

Noah chuckled, 'It was certainly my favourite yet!' he agreed, 'though, strictly speaking, it's not our first kiss…'

This point was lost on Marie who was already angling for another embrace. They kissed again, many times, until at last Noah suggested they try to get some sleep. He offered Marie the use of the bathroom first, and she reluctantly agreed, not keen to move from her snugly position next to him.

'But wouldn't you like us to…' Marie began, coyly, stroking her leg up and down his, their jeans creating a rough friction.

'No!' Noah interjected quickly, sitting up to break the physical connection between them, 'I mean, yes, of course, what man wouldn't? But no, not tonight, not when I've just found you again. There'll be plenty of time, hopefully, for that in the future… But the kisses? Yes, let's have lots more of those!'

And he took her lips with an unbridled passion that heated the space around them once more.

Marie felt like she was on fire. Her whole body, every nerve-ending alight. *Why does he have to be such a gentleman?* She asked herself, though she knew deep-down that she'd be very grateful for his restraint in the cool light of morning.

Having showered and dressed in the 'I Love Boston' T-shirt she'd bought from the hotel souvenir kiosk, Marie snuggled down in her own bed. Coming out of the bathroom in his underwear, Noah came over, running his hand down her face and kissing her sweetly on the forehead.

'Sleep tight, Gorgeous,' he said, before retreating under his own blankets.

Marie smiled contentedly to herself, happy in the knowledge that Christmas had come early for her this year, and her own, personal, jolly Santa was snoring away in the bed next to her! *Hopefully,* she thought as she dozed off, *the snow won't allow the planes to leave for at least another twenty-four hours!*

ABOUT THE AUTHOR

Rachel Hutchins lives in northeast England with her husband and three children. She works as a freelance proofreader and editor at ITP Proofreading and loves writing romance books. Her favourite place is walking along the local coastline.

As well as her contemporary stories under this name, Rachel also writes sweet historical romance under the pen name Anne Hutchins.

You can connect with Rachel and sign up to her newsletter via her website at www.authorrachelhutchins.com

Alternatively, she has social media pages on,

Facebook: www.facebook.com/rahutchinsauthor

Instagram: www.instagram.com/ra_hutchins_author

Twitter: www.twitter.com/hutchinsauthor

R. A. Hutchins

OTHER BOOKS BY R. A. HUTCHINS

The Angel and the Wolf

What do a beautiful recluse, a well-trained husky, and a middle-aged biker have in common?
Find out in this poignant story of love and hope!

When Isaac meets the Angel and her Wolf, he's unsure whether he's in Hell or Heaven.
Worse still, he can't remember taking that final step.
They say that calm follows the storm, but will that be the case for Isaac?

Fate has led him to her door,
Will she have the courage to let him in?

To Catch A Feather (Found in Fife Book One)

When tragedy strikes an already vulnerable Kate Winters, she retreats into herself, broken and beaten.
Existing rather than living, she makes a journey North to try to find herself, or maybe just looking for some sort of closure.

Cameron McAllister has known his own share of grief and love lost.
His son, Josh, is now his only priority.
In his forties and running a small coffee shop in a tiny Scottish fishing village, Cal knows he is unlikely to find love again.

When the two meet and sparks fly, can they overcome their past losses and move on towards a shared future, or are the memories which haunt them still too real?

A story of hope and longing, of despair and doubt, can Kate and Cal find their happily ever after?

Both books can be found on Amazon worldwide in e-book and paperback formats, as well as free to read on Kindle Unlimited.

R. A. Hutchins

HISTORICAL ROMANCE
BY ANNE HUTCHINS

Finding Love on Cobble Wynd

A small coastal town in North Yorkshire is the setting for these three romantic stories, all set in 1910.

As love blossoms for the residents of Lillymouth, figures from their past, mystery and danger all play a part in their story.

Will the course of true love run smooth, or is it not all plain sailing for these three ordinary couples?

Lose yourself in these sweet tales of loves lost and found:

The Little Library on Cobble Wynd

Considered firmly on the shelf, Bea comes to the Lilly Valley looking for a fresh start. She finds more companionship than she ever hoped for in Aaron and his young daughter, but is heartbreak hiding on the horizon?

A Bouquet of Blessings on Cobble Wynd

When florist Eve discovers that her blossoming attraction for the local vicar may be mutual, she is shocked when his attentions run cold. Could danger be lurking in the shadows?

Love is the Best Medicine on Cobble Wynd

An unexpected visitor turns Doctor William Allen's world upside down and sets his pulse racing in this tale of unwanted betrothal.

A standalone novel, with happily-ever-afters guaranteed, these are the first of many adventures on Cobble Wynd!

Available on Amazon worldwide in e-book and paperback formats, as well as free to read on Kindle Unlimited.

R. A. Hutchins

Printed in Great Britain
by Amazon